Sing Sarah Sing

Marla Shaw O'Neill

Second printing June 4, 2018
By Marla Shaw O'Neill

Sing Sarah Sing

Printed in the United States of America
Published by CreateSpace.com and Amazon.com

ISBN-978-0692276983
ISBN-069227698X

Cover graphics and photo editing by Bob O'Neill
Angel Song and Lyrics by Marla Shaw O'Neill
Composed by Bob O'Neill

Unless otherwise indicated, all Scripture Quotations are taken from the Holy Bible, The King James Version, Public Domain

To purchase other books by the author

Visit: www.amazon.com and Kindle

ACKNOWLEDGMENTS

I want to give a very special thank you to my husband, Robert (Bob) J. O'Neill, the love of my life, without your expertise and persistence I could not have finished this story. My heart is filled with such respect and gratitude for the tremendous help you gave me throughout this entire project. The timeless effort you spent putting the notes down on paper for the music to the Angle Song, and for playing your violin. I love you baby, thank you.

I want to say thank you to my mother Pearl J. Holman for her insight and encouragement who has been a huge help in my completing Sing Sarah Sing and for taking the time to read the draft. You never let me give up, you cheered me on. Thanks mom.

Thank you to Dorothy O'Neill for reading the draft and for your input, you're a sweet and endearing mom.

Thank you to Wanda Brazell, who sang the Angel Song with me, and thanks to the First Church of the Nazarene in Tallahassee, Florida, for allowing us to sing the Angel Song, in your church. Thank you to Annette Pevy for playing the piano and helping to compose the accompaniment. Pastor Dave and Anita Pullen, Pastors of the Church, we appreciate you and your congregation for listening to the Angel Song, you are all a blessing. Dana Brazell I want to thank you for playing the clarinet, you're amazing; Andrea Brazell and Rob Brazell on the sound system and David Brazell videotaping us. And to Shannon O'Neill, who inspires me with the passion she has for books, thank you. What a privilege to share our dream with you all.

Thanks to Pauline Morgan, a beautiful soul. Candy Ball my lifelong friend who's been a sister to me. Grace Gamble one of the most humble and God fearing women I've ever known, thank you for

Sing Sarah Sing

Printed in the United States of America
Published by CreateSpace.com and Amazon.com

ISBN-978-0692276983
ISBN-069227698X

Cover graphics and photo editing by Bob O'Neill
Angel Song and Lyrics by Marla Shaw O'Neill
Composed by Bob O'Neill

Unless otherwise indicated, all Scripture Quotations are taken from the Holy Bible, The King James Version, Public Domain

To purchase other books by the author

Visit: www.amazon.com and Kindle

ACKNOWLEDGMENTS

I want to give a very special thank you to my husband, Robert (Bob) J. O'Neill, the love of my life, without your expertise and persistence I could not have finished this story. My heart is filled with such respect and gratitude for the tremendous help you gave me throughout this entire project. The timeless effort you spent putting the notes down on paper for the music to the Angle Song, and for playing your violin. I love you baby, thank you.

I want to say thank you to my mother Pearl J. Holman for her insight and encouragement who has been a huge help in my completing Sing Sarah Sing and for taking the time to read the draft. You never let me give up, you cheered me on. Thanks mom.

Thank you to Dorothy O'Neill for reading the draft and for your input, you're a sweet and endearing mom.

Thank you to Wanda Brazell, who sang the Angel Song with me, and thanks to the First Church of the Nazarene in Tallahassee, Florida, for allowing us to sing the Angel Song, in your church. Thank you to Annette Pevy for playing the piano and helping to compose the accompaniment. Pastor Dave and Anita Pullen, Pastors of the Church, we appreciate you and your congregation for listening to the Angel Song, you are all a blessing. Dana Brazell I want to thank you for playing the clarinet, you're amazing; Andrea Brazell and Rob Brazell on the sound system and David Brazell videotaping us. And to Shannon O'Neill, who inspires me with the passion she has for books, thank you. What a privilege to share our dream with you all.

Thanks to Pauline Morgan, a beautiful soul. Candy Ball my lifelong friend who's been a sister to me. Grace Gamble one of the most humble and God fearing women I've ever known, thank you for reading the draft. And, Sheryl Collins you're a kindred spirit for sure, thank you for taking the time to meet with Bob and me.

Thanks to my sons and their wives. Mark & Angelica Liverio, (Joelma) and Jason Liverio, Abram and Mary Liverio and Jonathan Liverio who inspire me every day, and teach me, children are a true blessing from God. Thank you to my granddaughters Esperanza Liverio a bright star, and Olivia Liverio my sweet princess. Thanks to Bryan and Braden Brazell two precious little men of great potential and upcoming men of God. And thank you little Carlos a sweetie pie. I also want to thank my beautiful sister Barbara Shaw Ramirez whom I share many childhood memories with and who is one of the most intelligent people I know (you keep us straight.)

Thanks to Clyde Holman who passed away in 2010, he was a wonderful person and the love of my mother's life, her true soul mate. We miss you. It was in your home where Sing Sarah Sing was first conceived. I know you're fishing with the angels now.

Thanks to my guardian angels, who watch over me every day of my life and who speak God's truth into my heart and protect me and point me to Jesus.

I also want to say, I have found a treasure and mentor in an author I have looked up to and respected for many years. Her name is Bodie Thoene (pronounced Tay-nee). Her numerous, biblical, historical novels have given me years of encouragement and timeless insights into our precious Heavenly Father's Kingdom. On a daily basis I have read your posts Bodie, and have referenced your books many times. Your writing has brought joy, as well as tears into my life with always a lesson learned. Thank you for all you do. I am honored to call you friend. (Read Bodie's books they are life changing.)

But most of all I want to say, thank you Father God; Jesus, the son of God; and the precious Holy Spirit; for loving me and showing me the way, the truth and the life, as I travel on this journey home. Without you I could not have written this story. Thank you for the story, Sing Sarah Sing and for the Angel Song. You are always by my side and someday, I'll be going home on angels wings. But until that time I will keep the faith and follow the course you have laid out for me. I give you praise and honor and glory in your Holy Name. Amen.

This story is dedicated to:

Jesus, the son of God!

Sing to the Lord a new song; Sing to the Lord, all the earth. Sing to the Lord, praise His name. Proclaim His salvation day after day. Declare His glory among the nations, His marvelous deeds among all peoples.

Psalm 96

The Man in the Suit

Oh that You would bless me indeed, and enlarge my territory,
that Your hand would be with me, and that You would keep me from
evil, and that I might not cause pain. I Chronicles 4:10
(The Prayer of Jabez)

It was the morning of June 28, 1956, the air was stifling hot, 101 degrees and it wasn't even noon yet. School was over and summer vacation had begun. With summertime here and kids out of school, there would be picnics, swimming down at the lake and fishing 'til all hours of the night and day. Norma Jean, in her early morning routine was mopping the kitchen floor; sweat pouring from her brow, she sensed something in the air, expectancy of some kind. She had no idea what it could be, but she was about to find out. Lost in her thoughts, pushing the mop back and forth across the linoleum floor, she heard Sarah yelling.

"Granny, Granny," Sarah said, "Someone's here."

A man dressed in a black suit grinned at Sarah and blew his horn. Yelling from his car window he said, "Is it safe to get out of the car?"

1

Sounds of alarm and terror came from Taffy, Sarah's dog. "A stranger has arrived, beware." Taffy jumping and backing up barked non-stop.

Sarah was awe struck as she saw the shiny new car pull into the yard. It was a Ford, baby blue and white, Fairlane, with chrome trim and white-wall tires. But she didn't recognize the man.

"I wonder who that could be." Sarah thought. I don't know anyone with a shiny new car." Sarah looked at the man, then at the car, and then towards the porch.

"Taffy, hush up!" Granny scolded, standing at the screen door looking to see who was there. "Sarah, take Taffy to the back yard." Granny said with a hint of irritation in her voice, then stepped onto the porch for a better look.

"Yes ma'am. Come on Taffy. Come on girl, let's go; come on." As Sarah began to run, Taffy followed running and jumping about, not caring who the man was. Taffy was thrilled that she was going to play with her best friend and nothing else mattered. Taffy a golden retriever loves to play and has an enthusiastic, boisterous personality. Protector of her master she was friendly, but strangers beware. Curious and playful she often gets herself into a lot of trouble without meaning too!

"That's a good girl." Sarah said as she picked up a stick throwing it past Taffy. "Bring it here girl!" Taffy ran after the stick as if to say, "OK let's play," as was her nature. She brought the stick back to Sarah giving her several kisses. Sarah cuddled with the dog then said, "Be good now girl I don't have time to play." Head down and tail between her legs Taffy inched her way over to Sarah. Sarah bent down, held her by the collar, and tied her to the little dog house. Taffy jumped around and barked as if to say, "Come on back I want to play." Sarah gave her a pat on the head then ran back around the house, as she did she saw the man get out of the car, pick Granny up, and swing her around. Granny was laughing and hugged him back. It was her brother George whom she hadn't seen for many years.

"George is it really you?" Granny stood there her hand over her chest. Mouth open and wide eyed. "I can't believe it." "What are you doing here? It's been so long." A million questions went through her mind as she stood looking at her brother. "Where's Betty and the kids?" she thought.

George stood mischievously, like a little school boy for a moment, knowing he had surprised her. Then he reached out to give her a big hug and said, "Yes Norma Jean it's really me." Laughing he said. "I got a letter from Cousin Bea in Huntsville asking me to come see everyone so I thought it would be a good idea. You know how it is with farming from sun-up to sun-down, and raising the kids I never had time to visit. But here I am. Where's Bernie?" George asked looking around for his brother-in-law.

"George, Bernie passed away last March. He went in his sleep real peaceful like. I do miss the ole jackrabbit; we had some wonderful years together." Granny said feeling the loss grip her heart remembering her husband, not letting George see her pain.

"Norma Jean I'm so sorry to hear that. I should have come sooner. George sighed and said, "Time got away from me. I wish

3

things had been different. If we had lived closer they would have. You would have enjoyed my kids. They're all grown up now with kids of their own. I have pictures I'll show you later. Last spring the farm burned down. Betty had a stroke and passed away a year ago. After she passed I was alone and really didn't have a need to stay there anymore. The truth is, I was praying one evening and it was as if, the Lord said to me, "It's time to go see your sister, Norma Jean." So here I am. How are you doing? Are you in good health?" George asked looking concerned.

Granny smiled at her big brother and said. "I'm fine. Come on in the house. I'll fix you a glass of sweet tea. We've got some catching up to do."

George walked towards the house and as he did he reminisced about the good old days.

The white farm-house was trimmed with red shutters. Two weathered rockers graced the porch. He imagined Granny and Sarah sitting there in the afternoons, waving to everyone that passed by. The mountains were cooler in the evenings making it more comfortable to sit and rock, lazy summer days were like that.

"I remember how beautiful the sun-sets are, in the evenings." George said as he stood for a few moments looking around.

"Yes they are." Granny said. "Sarah loves to sit here with me and listen to stories about how I grew up. She calls them used-to, days. I guess because I go around saying I used to…" They both snickered.

"I remember how good of a story teller you are sis, I miss that time together. I especially remember the one about *Jonny, I want my liver back*. I still can't get to sleep when I think about that one." George laughed, looking down at his little sister. "Time sure has flown."

They both laughed out loud as they threw their heads back and cackled like a couple of chickens.

"I see you still keep elephant ears growing next to the porch." George said nodding towards the plants, as he climbed the steps of the porch.

"Yes and Sarah uses them for umbrellas when it rains just like we used to do. See what I mean…used to!" Granny said pulling her apron back and forth fanning her chest, wiping at the sweat beneath her dress.

"You always had the prettiest flowers." George said looking around at the white and pink azaleas; yellow and orange marigolds; that bordered the other three sides of the porch. "I see you still have rosebushes. The pink, white and yellow ones are my favorite." They were Norma Jean's pride and joy she planted then in the center of the yard.

"Yes but the red ones produced the sweetest fragrance; I have those growing outside my bedroom window." Granny said pointing to the back of the house.

George turned, taking in the front yard, lost in thought as he stared. An old oak tree full of moss stood as if guarding the place; it must have been at least one hundred years old. It stood tall and full next to the road giving shade to little concrete chickens and ducks. A birdbath adorned the yard as well, where birds chirped and splashed and Bubba the old tomcat, crouched behind the tree, hoping for a meal. Periwinkles of white and lavender grew under the old oak.

Granny catching his eyes said, "Sarah spends many summer days playing under that old oak." She says her mighty steed is that tire-swing that's hanging from the tree. I've seen her climb to the very top, many times to survey her little kingdom."

The neighborhood has grown quite a bit. There are homes spread out over the valley with a couple that are just over the ridge to the west. Except for Susie, her house is right behind ours.

As George stood there on the porch he reached for the screen door and held it open for Granny. Glancing around he said, "Well, it sure brings back a lot of memories. Where have all the years gone; twenty to be exact."

"Some things have changed but not too much." Granny said opening the screen door. "We replaced the shingle roof and installed indoor plumbing, a few years back, thank the Lord for that. I couldn't stand those freezing mornings going to the outhouse in the middle of the night. The old well still works though. I use it to water the chickens and keep the garden moist." Granny chuckled as she thought about the trips to the outhouse and said, "Thank the Lord for modern conveniences."

"I hear ya sis." said George.

Entering the house George could see that the living room was simple yet comfortable. He smelled fresh cut roses, he saw them from the living room they were sitting in mason jars on the kitchen table that was made of red Formica, with chrome legs. Light filtered into the room through the kitchen window that was over the sink, where a little pot of violets set upon the windowsill. He could see through the kitchen window a spectacular view of mountains, various trees and a rolling landscape of farmland.

An overstuffed chair sat in one corner of the living room along with a mahogany camel-backed sofa, with floral print of deep green and rose which sat in front of a large bay window. The windows were draped with ivory colored lace, tied back with green satin bows.

He looked around the room and sitting on antique end tables that were at each end of the sofa, were two lamps with pink shades, adorned with tiny crystals that made rainbows dance on the wall. In front of the fireplace, now empty of ash and flames, sat a braided rug which covered the living room floor where a tomcat sat curled, napping. Granny was an immaculate house keeper; the floor was scrubbed and polished. "Just like mama, Norma Jean the floor is so clean I could eat off of it." George said still taking in the room.

A mantle carved from oak, hung above the fireplace with pictures of their mama and papa; and Sarah; and her mother, Jenny.

"Jenny was a beautiful girl, it's a shame Sarah never got to know her, dying in childbirth and all." George got real melancholy. "Leaving you to raise her alone I'm sorry I didn't help you more, Sis. And the tragedy of her father being murdered the day after she was born it's an awful shame. I'm so sorry Norma Jean."

"Well, life is messy most of the time. Granny said. Changing the subject she said, "Come on in the kitchen George and have a seat. I'll get you a nice glass of sweet iced tea. There'll be time to talk about old times later." Granny said as she reached to turn on a small electric fan.

The breeze caused the red and white checked curtains to blow in and out of the kitchen window. There was a soft hum as the fan blew, making the room a little more bearable in the stifling heat.

A needle point of Jesus in the garden, hung on one kitchen wall. And on the other wall were two stitcheries. One was, "Home Sweet Home." And the other one was, "God Bless Our Home."

"Thank you Norma Jean. They say this is going to be a hot summer." George said taking a seat. He sat very still for a moment listening to Sarah as she played softly on the piano from the front room.

Sarah had a natural talent for music and could play any instrument, her favorite was the piano. Granny had bought her one from a second hand store. She spent most of her waking hours practicing. Her passion was playing the piano and singing. George was in awe as he listened to her play. He understood now why the Lord had directed him there.

Taking an ice pick Granny opened the icebox and began to chop ice to put in George's glass. She poured the tea over the ice and added some lemon then handed it to George. Stirring a pot of beans that was cooking on the stove she checked to see if the chicken and dressing, was done. An apple pie sat cooling on the windows ledge.

"Sure does smell good in here Norma Jean, it's been a while since I've had a real home cooked meal. I try, but I'm not a very good cook." George said. He stood up, took off his sports coat and hung it over the back of his chair. He stuck his thumbs under his red suspenders, and snapped them. He rolled his shirt sleeves up, breathed in deeply and sat down.

He then picked up his glass and took a long cool drink. "Boy that's good. You make the best sweet tea in all of Alabama." George said enjoying the cold fluid going down his throat. Even though the windows were open and the fan was blowing, he felt hot and sticky. He didn't mind though, he took out his red bandana, wiped his face and forehead, and waited for Granny to join him. He was on a mission and wanted her full attention.

"So George, what's this all about?" Granny asked as she sat down at the table wiping her hands on her apron then taking a sip of her tea.

"Well sis, ever since I was a little boy I dreamed of writing songs and traveling around the country. You might think that's strange, me being a farmer and all; but there's a creative side to me that I want to explore." George said taking another drink.

"No I don't think it's strange at all George. I remember you entering a contest when we were kids. You won first place in the *Best Original Music Award in the State of Alabama* competition. I was so proud of you. I still have the newspaper article around here somewhere. You were the talk of the town for a long time. Sorry I interrupted please go on." Granny turned to listen more intently.

9

"Right after Betty died it seemed like my whole life ended. Both my kids and their families live out of state. Matt and Jackie have two children. Stevie was ten and Susie was eight at the time. Sandy and Dave have twins, Kevin and Terry. They were three years old. They all had their hands full. I didn't want to disrupt their lives. Then, the house burned down and I was devastated. I lived in the barn for months. There was no one else to worry about, and so it didn't bother me to stay in the barn. In fact, it was a God-send although I didn't realize it at the time. I cooked my meals outside on an open fire. Went down to the creek and caught fish, set traps for rabbits. I slept in perfect peace under the stars. I hadn't thought about writing for years. Oh from time to time, it would cross my mind but I just let it go.

Then one night I listened to the night sounds. The birds and crickets were actually serenading me. I pulled out an old note pad and began to write this song. I believe the angels were singing it to me as I wrote it down. Afterwards, all my anxiety and hurt was gone.

> *Though times are hard*
> *I'm by your side*
> *Your tears I hold within my hand*
> *No matter what I'll hold you close*
> *Look to the one who understands.*
> *Though fears may come and tears may fall*
> *Be still and know that I am God*
> *Let perfect peace restore your heart*
> *And know my love we'll never part*

Chorus:

I walked the road of trials and torment

I sat with those who love me still

But on the cross I felt the suffering of all the ones who

love me most.

The birds they sing a nightly chorus

Of joy and peace to all they bring

So lift your voice and head toward heaven

And learn their song, their song and sing.

He gives me peace, He gives me life, the angels sing be

glorified

Praise to the King our mighty King

We're going home on angels wings.

"George, that is beautiful!" Tears streamed down Granny's face as she listened to the ballad of a man who knew pain.

"One more verse Norma Jean." George said as he continued to sing.

When in the stillness now at midnight

I see the star of love so bright

I'll never ever doubt my Savior

For He will lead me through the night

And on the breeze I hear Him whisper...

Press on my child and do not weep

For at the dawn you'll have your answer

So close your eyes and go to sleep.

Chorus:

I walked the road of trials and torment

I sat with those who love me still

But on the cross I felt the suffering of all the ones who

love me most.

The birds they sing a nightly chorus

Of joy and peace to all they bring

So lift your voice and head toward heaven

And learn their song, their song and sing.

He gives me peace, He gives me life, the angels sing be

glorified

Praise to the King our mighty King

We're going home on angels wings.

By the time George had finished singing the song Granny was down on her knees. Crying and praying. She couldn't explain it but all the heartache and pain she had been carrying vanished. She felt as light as a feather and started laughing. She got up, threw her arms up in the air and danced around the whole kitchen praising and glorifying God.

"George! George!" Granny stammered trying to talk to George but she couldn't speak in English. She was talking in a funny language. Taffy ran to the screen door to see what all the fuss was about. George looked through blurry eyes as tears spilled and ran down his face, he felt his heart fill with joy knowing he was in the presence of the Lord.

Sarah came to the doorway standing and watching, her mouth a gap, she stared in wonderment. "What in the world is going on?" She thought.

After a few minutes, things settled down and Granny was able to speak where she could be understood. "Thank you Jesus, praise you Lord."

"Granny, what was that? Are you alright?" Sarah asked not understanding what just happened.

"Sarah I'll have to explain it to you later. It's a beautiful thing being in the company of the Lord and speaking to Him in His language. It'll take a little time to explain and I'll need to get the Bible to show you what it's all about. Be patient for now sweetheart I promise, I'll explain everything to you later. Granny said still feeling the effects of the song.

"OK Granny." Sarah said but was very curious. She sat down thoughts rushing through her mind but said nothing else.

Uncle George and Granny giggled and praised the Lord. Then Granny said, "We are drinking from the wells of Jesse. We've tasted the new wine from heaven." They did a little jig together. They were acting like two little kids.

"New wine!" Sarah thought. "Where'd they get wine? That must be why Granny wants to wait to tell me. I'm too young for wine." Sarah listened intently as she watched her Granny and her uncle enjoy their time together.

The Proposition

Lord, thou hast been our dwelling place in all generations.
Psalm 90:1

Granny sat down to catch her breath. George kept feasting on the manna from heaven. A gush of laughter exploded within him and great sounds came from him like a trumpet that had been stopped up for years. Joy had erupted, and was sent straight from the throne room of heaven. The angels rejoiced at the sound of revival in two people that needed it most.

"George, that song is anointed." Granny said trying to compose herself. "You need to get it recorded so that everyone who hears it can be blessed. God's hand is on it for sure and he'd be glorified in a mighty way." Granny said still basking in the effects of the Holy Spirit.

George's eyes were sparkling with excitement as he said, "That's what I came to talk to you about. I know Sarah is only ten years old, but Cousin Beatrice raved in her letter, over the anointing that's on Sarah's voice." George quaked and kept on talking, "I

14

would like for her to sing the song in Tennessee at a recording studio. I've already spoken to a friend of mine about Sarah and the song, and he wants to hear her sing."

Grinning George cleared his throat and said. "I'd sing it but my voice isn't the same as it used to be. There's that used to be again, giving Granny a wink. "It cracks and becomes a little hoarse after a while. And besides that, God specifically said He wants Sarah to sing the song."

Granny looked at him as if she had been knocked off her feet. She knew this song was a gift from God. "It certainly is anointed." Granny said her eyes taking on the look of a lioness watching her new born cup as she said. "George this is truly astonishing. Sarah and I have both been praying that God would open doors for her to share her gift. I've known since she was two years old that her voice was a gift from the Good Lord. Every time she'd sing tiny little waves would wash over my soul and the hairs on my body would stand straight up from my head, down to my toes... She has sung at school functions and Church gatherings and every time she sings God moves on the people's hearts." Granny's voice was firm and determined she was full of power and conviction as she spoke. She knew God was going to use her granddaughter to minister in music.

George looked at Granny and said, "I haven't heard her sing except for that little bit a few minutes ago it sent chills all over me. I can't wait to hear more.

When Cousin Bea wrote to me about Sarah's amazing voice, I figured Sarah would be the perfect one to sing the song. Now I know she's the one. It's called, *The Angel song. Who better to sing it than an angel?"*

"So what do you think Norma Jean?" asked George.

Granny looked at George then at Sarah and asked, "Do you think you could sing Uncle George's song Sarah?" Granny knew Sarah could, she just wanted to hear it from her.

Without hesitation Sarah looked at them both and said, "Of course I can. Hum the tune for me again and I'll sing it right now." Sarah was not shy when it came to singing.

Granny looked at Sarah thinking about Sarah's mama. She thought, "She's the spitting image of her mother except for the color of her skin. Sarah had thick, long dark blond curls that framed her oval face which was a light caramel brown. Her eyes were as blue as a clear summer sky. And when she smiled, it was, as if heaven sent a sunbeam shooting out from her eyes sending warm, and inviting hugs to your heart. She had a small dimple in her right cheek, accenting her sweet face that transformed her into an angelic being. Her heart was pure and unassuming. But there was also a hint of mischief in her demeanor that made her even more loveable. And when she'd flash that smile and tilt her head you knew something was up. She was definitely a soul to remember. Sarah had a tremendous challenge though and it would haunt her all of her life. Sarah's father, whom she had never known was a black man. And in 1956, that was not acceptable in the white man's world. White people and colored people didn't mix. And, if they did, trouble was paramount.

Among her many attributes she had a very distinct and special gift. It was her voice. It transcended all racial differences because when she sang everyone forgot about her color. She must have been mentored by the angels because the minute she opened her mouth to sing it was captivating. The birds stopped singing; all of heaven hushed, to listen to the melody of a soul in tune with God himself. It captured your heart to the point that all you could do was sit in total surrender; soaking up the angelic sound and never wanting to return from the magical land it took you too. Each note was clear and crisp, and always in perfect pitch. Her demeanor was calm yet confident. She sang and it lifted you to another dimension, the soul took flight never to return. This talent would take her on many adventures. She'd travel to foreign lands where she'd minister to many people of all races and color. Frightening, and exciting, it would be the fulfilling of her destiny. These thoughts ran through Norma Jean's mind as she looked at her granddaughter.

"George, sing the song for Sarah she'll take it from there." Granny said anticipating George's reaction. She couldn't wait for George to hear her granddaughter sing. She was proud of Sarah and knew without a doubt God had a special calling on her life.

Sarah listened intently, closed her eyes, and then felt all the emotions and love that came from the spirit of the song as George sang it for her.

She sat down at the piano, hummed the tune, and then began to sing. By the time she had finished George and Granny were both down on their knees crying and worshiping the only true King; Jesus the son of God.

George tried to compose himself as he spoke. "Norma Jean, Sarah has a powerful and almost hypnotizing voice. It takes you to a place that you never want to come back from. That was the most beautiful sound I've ever heard. Bea was certainly right when she told me about Sarah's talent and that she sang with conviction and feeling. It's like she becomes the song. George turned to Sarah you are truly an amazing little girl. The angels gave me the words to the song, but you gave them life."

"Thank you, Uncle George. I'm glad that it blessed you in such a special way. All the glory goes to the Lord. I don't take the gift he gave me for granted." said Sarah.

"That's true wisdom, Sarah." George said as he raised an eye brow, looking surprised then smiled. He thought to himself, "This little girl is the real deal."

George looked down at the floor, shook his head then looked at Norma Jean and said, "Oh my goodness, what a voice. Sarah is very talented she's perfect, everyone is going to love her."

Granny beamed with pride and said, "I told you she could sing. Now what did you want to ask me?"

George moved, with great emotion said, "Whew let me catch my breath. Just hear me out before you answer. I've been in contact with an old school mate of mine. He's pretty big in the music world. I told him about the song and what it means to me. He said if I would come see him and let him hear the song, he'd see what he could do. So with that being said, I came here to ask you if think it would be alright for Sarah to go with me, so she could sing the song for Mr. Berry? We'd probably be gone all summer. I know it's asking a lot but I really believe if he hears her sing, it'll be a hit."

Norma Jean looked at George with surprise and hesitation and said, "I'm not sure about that George a white man and a little girl like Sarah, there could be some problems. Let me pray about it and I'll give you an answer in the morning. And of course, Sarah would have to agree."

"What do you think Sarah?" Granny asked as she put her arm around her and squeezed real tight.

Heart racing, Sarah stood up; her voice squealed with excitement as she said, "I think it's going to be thrilling and swell. I love to sing especially when it makes people happy and blessed. When do we start?" Sarah was always ready for an adventure.

George looked at Sarah, chuckled out loud and said. "I knew you'd be agreeable. We'll need to wait and see what your grandma decides. And then I'll need to make some phone calls. We could be on the road by the end of the week."

Sarah could hardly believe her ears. This was one of the most exciting things that had ever happened to her. "OK Uncle George I'll wait to see what Granny says. I'll try to keep from shouting it to the world. I've got some thinking to do myself. I'll see ya later Uncle George, I'm going to go out back for a little while."

Heading out back Sarah was lost in thought, "If Granny says yes, I'll be on the road with my Uncle George singing and playing the music I love and it'll be on the radio!" Running and skipping she hummed a little tune. *"I've got the joy, joy, joy, joy down in my heart..."*

In the few hours that she had been with her Uncle George she felt a kindred spirit between them and trusted him completely. She hoped that Granny's answer would be yes.

As she sang the little tune, Sarah went to her favorite spot under a pecan tree in the back yard. There was an old stump that she sat on to contemplate and pray about big questions that would come up. Questions like who the cutest boy in school was and what was Susie Cooper doing talking to Betsy Clark? Where did birds sleep at night and what would Granny's decision be? She could hardly contain her excitement. As she sat there, Susie, her next door neighbor came running over to see her.

"SSSSarah!" Susie said, as she whistled, missing her two front teeth sounding like a snake in her soft whiney voice. "Who's car issss that in your front yard? Does your Granny have a beau?" Susie said, in a sing song way. She was very inquisitive always poking her nose where it did not belong.

"Gracious no!" Sarah said. "That's Granny's brother she hasn't seen him for twenty years." Sarah replied exasperated by Susie's questions.

"What'sss, he doing here?" Susie asked bluntly. Susie was also ten. Her plump body was supported by two stocky legs that looked too short for her large frame.

Exasperated and irritated Sarah looked to the sky, shook her head and thought, "Lord, give me grace." Then she said, "Well I can't say right now, I'll let you know tomorrow." Sarah enjoyed keeping her secrets from Susie, who was constantly putting her nose in everyone's business. The kids all had a saying, "Telegraph, telephone and tell Susie. She loved to spread gossip.

Susie gave a big humph and then in her whiney, whistling voice said. "Lotto, you better tell me or I'll ssssit here all day til you do."

"Suit yourself Susie I gotta go, see ya later." said Sarah.

Sarah went to the house then locked the door behind her. Susie was known to walk in your house unannounced. Sarah peeked out the window to see if Susie was really going to sit there all day.

Susie turned around and watched as Sarah left. Then she went running home to tell her mama who the stranger was. "Mama… guesssss what?" Susie ran into her house yelling.

"That Susie is never going to grow up I can't tell her anything," Sarah thought. "Why do people have to be so nosey?" Sarah went to her room she was excited yet a little apprehensive about her journey. Not quite sure what to expect.

Questions of the Heart

Before the mountains were brought forth, or ever thou hadst formed the earth and the world, even from everlasting to everlasting, thou art God. Psalm 90:2

Sarah did the only thing she knew to do in times like this she knelt by her bed and began to pray.

Lord, I'm just a little girl but I feel like I've been here for a very long time. I love that you trusted me with such a special gift and I long to share it with others. But Lord, sometimes people look at me funny and sometimes I hear them whisper behind my back. I know I'm different, I'm not black and I'm not white. Granny says you made me special for a reason but sometimes it hurts Lord. I never knew my mommy or my daddy and that's OK, because Granny is sweet and kind to me. But Lord, if you're not too busy and if you don't mind. Could you please help me understand why people are downright cruel at times? I'm pretty sure I'm going on a trip with Uncle George. Please help us do real good for you Lord and please help me to be brave. Amen

Granny was walking by Sarah's room and heard her praying. She poked her head in the room and said. "Sarah honey, can I come in?"

Sarah getting up from kneeling to pray sat down on the edge of her bed. "I guess you heard my prayer." Sarah said as she looked at the floor.

"Yes honey, I did. I know it's been hard for you but God has something extra big for your life and you have to be tough. You see, he sends these trials our way to help us become stronger. Life is hard and messy a lot of times so get prepared because you will have a long life and will need all the strength you can get. Don't take anything for granted. Be humble but also be wise and smart. You know what? You have two different nations you can minister to. Your piercing blue eyes will put people in their place and your voice will melt their hearts. Don't be afraid the good book says to be as wise as a serpent but harmless as a dove. If others don't accept you they are the ones who lose out not you. OK sweetheart?" Granny said compassionately.

Sarah stood up and gave Granny a great big hug and then gave her a kiss on the cheek, as she did she lingered for a moment then said. "It gets real hard sometimes the other kids call me Lotto short for mulatto. I looked it up in the dictionary it said it's something they call a person who has a white parent and a black parent." Sarah hung her head and got real quiet.

"Granny, do you think I'll ever be accepted for who I am and not for my color?" Sarah asked.

23

"Oh Sarah, I'm sorry you have to face this in your life but I promise it will make you stronger. Yes you had a white mother and a black father. But that is not your fault. I've learned in life to ignore ignorant people. They don't know any better. You'd think they would but they don't. I love you no matter what color you are; of course I'm your grandma. But I'll tell you this, your mother loved you more than you can imagine. She'd sit and sing to you and rub her hand over her stomach and call you her little princess. That's what the name Sarah means, you know?

I believe your daddy loved you too. They worked on Mr. Brown's cotton farm and in the evenings he'd walk your mother home. I guess one thing led to another and next thing I knew Jenny was pregnant with you. Of course we didn't know you were a girl at the time. I guess she knew in her heart that's what you'd be. And so when you were born and Jenny died I named you Sarah. That is what she would have wanted. Your father was found dead the day after you were born. They found him lying in a ditch no one knows who did it. I don't think we'll ever know. This isn't anything you should worry about. God has a way of working all things out in his time. Now you concentrate on your music and being a blessing to folks. God has big plans for you little princess." Granny spoke firm and from her heart to her granddaughter.

"Alright Granny, but could you please tell me about my daddy what his name was and where he lived? I'd sure like to know what he was like and maybe meet the family someday." Sarah said with a sigh.

Granny sat next to Sarah on her bed. "Sarah I don't know a lot about him but I know he was kind and a hard worker. I met his mother at the funeral he's buried in their family cemetery over near Sand Rock. His name was David Elijah Todd. They called him David. He also had the voice of an angel. I'm sure that's where you got your music ability. Jenny could draw beautifully and could make the most beautiful quilts but she didn't sing much except while she was carrying you. I kept the *Evan's* name for you because it made more since at the time since I was to be your legal guardian. I haven't seen Mrs. Todd for ten years. But if you want I'll take you to see her." Granny looked at Sarah and waited for her answer.

"I would like that very much Granny if you don't mind." Sarah held her breath then exhaled. Granny reached up and brushed the tears from Sarah's eyes.

"Alright I'll see if that will be alright with her and we'll go tomorrow." Granny stood up, picked up her dish cloth, and turned to go to the kitchen then said. "Now, decide what you'll need for your trip with Uncle George just in case the good Lord says it's OK for you to go." She stood there for a moment, flung the dishtowel over her shoulder then turned and left the room.

Looking in her closet Sarah counted two full skirts and a crinoline. She had three tops that would go with those. She'd wear her best clothes with her black patent leather Sunday shoes and white socks, for the audition and wear the black skirt and white blouse with her saddle oxfords for everyday wear.

Then she found an old carpet bag. "This will work." She thought and began packing.

"I sure hope the Lord tells Granny it is alright for me to go with Uncle George. He's a good man and I know he loves the Lord. You can see it in his face when he smiles." Sarah thought then began to sing as she packed. Peace settled over her then she heard Granny call that supper was ready.

"George, will you say grace?" Granny asked.

Bowing their heads George asked the Lord to bless the meal.

The Answer

Thou turnest man to destruction; and sayest, Return, ye children of men. Psalm 90:3

The next morning Sarah was eager to find out what Granny's decision would be. She went to the kitchen put the pot coffee on to perk, and then set the table for breakfast.

Granny looked up at Sarah and said, "Well aren't you the early bird? You act like you're expecting some news or something." Smiling, Granny turned her head knowing full well why Sarah was up so early.

Sarah, giddy with excitement lit up as she grinned and said, "I am, hoping, to hear some exciting news!"

George came in from outside. He scratched his head and looked at Norma Jean then at Sarah and asked, "What are you two up to?" As if he didn't know.

Granny sat down squinting at George with the look of a hawk zooming in on its prey and said, "George, I have to tell you. I have some reservations about letting Sarah go with you. I know we aren't to have a spirit of fear, but of love and power and a sound mind. I

27

prayed earnestly last night. I went to sleep and I had this dream. I dreamed I was flying all over Alabama, Georgia, and North Carolina and ended up in Tennessee. I saw a lot of lights and people gathering together. Then I came to this huge sanctuary. I heard music coming from inside. I went to the door then walked inside and there on the platform was Sarah. She was surrounded by people playing all kinds of musical instruments it was beautiful. She was singing *How Great Thou Art!* I couldn't tell how many people were there but I'd guess about 5000 were in the audience. There were three balconies, every seat was taken. I stood in wonder and amazement. The people began to weep and stand to their feet, raised their hands toward heaven, and began running to the front of the sanctuary. As they did they were knocked down by an unseen power. And then God spoke to my heart. *He said, "Norma Jean for this purpose Sarah was sent and you should not stop her. I am with her and will lead and guide her. I will be with her and use her for my glory to save many souls. Don't be afraid to let her go."*

"I know this dream is an answer to my prayer," Granny said. "And I don't want to do anything to displease the Lord so the answer is, yes, Sarah can go with you."

George was dumb struck. He stared and couldn't speak for a moment. He was hopeful she'd say yes, but her dream was a big surprise, it was prophetic.

Sarah, jumped up, hugged her Granny and said, "I knew it! I knew God would say yes." Then she hugged Uncle George.

George smiling and happy said, "OK, well, ah, I guess I'll make the necessary phone calls and let them know we will be coming. Thank you Jesus, and thank you Norma Jean." George was ecstatic to know that God and Norma Jean said yes. That confirmed to him this journey was truly of the Lord.

"Granny is it alright if I go down to Beth's house to tell her I'm going on a trip to sing on the radio?" Sarah said and could hardly contain her excitement.

Beth had been Sarah's best friend all her life. Sarah was born on June 18, 1946; at 12:15 a.m. and Beth Montgomery had been born at the exact same time. They were now 10 years old. Beth was tall and slender her fiery green eyes and long lashes, could stop you in your tracks. Red bushy curls lay over her shoulders which she let run wild most of the time. When she smiled there were dimples on each cheek and enough freckles to fill a pepper jar. As a matter of fact that is exactly what Sarah called her, *"freckles"*. She had a temper that was as hot as chili peppers. Sarah was the only one that could get away with calling her that though. If anyone else tried it, she'd box 'em in the eye. She hated her freckles, that is, until one day at school they had a freckle contest. The one with the most freckles won a free ice cream soda down at Toby's Ice-cream parlor and a five dollar bill. Beth won and from then on she was proud of her freckles. Sarah envied her even more, because underneath those pepper specks was beautiful fair skin.

"Yes Sarah." Granny said. "After we eat breakfast you can go see Beth and ask her mom if she wouldn't mind, to come down

29

and see me this afternoon." Granny said putting a plate of scrambled eggs on the table.

After breakfast Sarah hurried to Beth's house she couldn't wait to tell her the news. Beth was still in her pajamas when she heard her mom call from down stairs that Sarah was here to see her.

"Go on up there Sarah." Mrs. Montgomery said as she folded towels she had brought in from off the clothes line.

"Thanks Mrs. M. Oh, I almost forgot, Granny would like you to go see her this afternoon if you can." Sarah said running up the stairs.

"I believe I can do that." Mrs. M said. Watching as Sarah ran up the stairs. "My goodness she must have something important to discuss with Beth this morning." Mrs. M. thought.

Sarah burst into Beth's bedroom and said, "Beth, get dressed I have some exciting news to tell you lets go down by the lake, bring your cut offs so we can go swimming."

Beth stretched real big, yawned then jumped up and went to the bathroom to get dressed. Sarah waited in anticipation.

As Beth came back into the room Sarah said, "You need to do something with your hair. Let me braid it for you."

"OK but hurry up Sarah I can't wait to hear about this exciting news that you woke me up for." Beth said, sitting down at her vanity table for Sarah to braid her hair.

"Ow not so tight Sarah," Beth chided. I don't want to look like I've been in a tug of war with my hair on one side, and you on the other. Your gona make me look Chinese.

Sarah laughed and said, "Well you won't have to take it down for a day or two after this." "There I'm done."

Beth pulled at her braids trying to loosen them a little. "All right I'm ready, let's go."

They ran down the stairs to the kitchen grabbed some apples and chips and put them in a paper sack. They also grabbed a couple of buttered biscuits that Beth's mom had baked that morning; then out the back door they went.

"See ya later mom we're going to the lake." Beth yelled to her mom on her way out.

"See ya later Mrs. M." Sarah echoed.

They ran and skipped the whole way to the lake laughing and giggling and singing a silly song. *"Lulu where are you going, upstairs to take a bath...Lulu with legs like tooth picks...and a neck like a giraffe...Lulu stepped in the bath tub, Lulu pulled out the plug...Oh my goodness, Oh my soul...there goes Lulu down the whole...LUUUULUUUU....glob, glob!"* The girls laughed feeling completely happy and carefree.

Puffy white clouds were scattered around the blue sky and as they walked along the trail they saw an eagle soaring, looking for some unsuspecting prey, maybe a mouse or a rabbit. In the distance a baby doe looked up startled, stood very still and then ran off into the woods. As they got closer to the lake they heard voices. It was Tommy and Jimmy splashing around in the water. They were best friends and had tormented Sarah and Beth for as long as they could remember, of course it went both ways. Beth loved to get even.

31

Sarah ducked behind a tree. "Shh," she whispered, "Beth, don't let them see us." But Beth kept on walking. She saw an opportunity to get even with the boys and nothing was going to stop her.

"Well, well, well, what do we have here?" Beth asked watching the boys startled faces, completely taken off guard. "What do you think you're doing?" Beth yelled as she stood at the edge of the lake with a mischievous look on her face.

Tommy and Jimmy were in the water butt naked they didn't think anyone would be down at the lake at this time of day. They looked up at the same time and saw Beth standing on the bank holding a stick out over the water with their clothes dangling at the other end.

"Beth Montgomery you put those clothes down and get out of here." Tommy yelled, red faced with anger and embarrassment. Jimmy ducked under the water for a few minutes hoping they'd leave but realizing he couldn't hold his breath forever came back up for air and yelled.

"Yeah, Freckles put our clothes down right now. I'm gonna tell your mama when I get out of here."

"Well, then come on and make me Jim-Bo." Beth said laughing hysterically as she walked away unintimidated.

"Come on Beth, don't leave us like this." The boys pleaded. They saw Sarah peeking from around the tree.

"What? Lotto is with you too?" Tommy screamed.

"For that Tommy, I'm gonna throw your clothes in the tar pit." Beth yelled turning to run away.

"Come on Sarah let's get out of here." Beth grabbed Sarah's hand and started to run.

"Beth stop, you can't take their clothes, how will they get home? They'll be naked." Sarah tried to reason with Beth.

"Yeah Beth, we'll get you for this." Jimmy called in desperation.

"Well it serves them right for calling you Lotto." Beth was mad. "Apologize right now or I'll dump your clothes in the water!" Beth was red faced and meant what she said.

"OK, OK!" Both boys said with all sincerity. "We're sorry Sarah we won't call you Lotto again. Come on Beth bring our clothes back." Tommy said being truly sorry.

Beth still holding the clothes on the end of the stick brought them back and held them out over the water again.

"I shouldn't give them back to you but since you apologized here catch." Beth let the stick drop.

"No, no, Beth, wait!" Tommy and Jimmy dog paddled over to catch their clothes, but Beth let them drop from the stick, laughing as she ran away.

"BETH!" They both yelled. "We'll get you for this." The boys were furious. Beth and Sarah ran away laughing hysterically.

The girls were out of breath when they reached the old cave where they often went to share their secrets.

"Beth that was the funniest thing I've ever seen. Did you see the looks on their faces? Eyes wide and pleading, their faces turned as red as a beet. There's no way they'll ever tell anyone about that. It is too humiliating." Sarah said, bent over with laughter.

"They're so mean all the time. I couldn't resist, I had to do it." Beth said still trying to catch her breath.

Calming down she asked, "Now what is this exciting news you wanted to tell me?"

Sarah sat down on a large rock that was sitting inside the opening of the cave. They never went very far inside because they had heard ghost stories and didn't want to take any chances. They kept a lantern in the old cave for times such as this.

Beth lit the lantern. Sarah said, "Whew I'm still trying to get over the look on their faces." The girls started to laugh again. "They sure were mad." Sarah said sitting on the rock as she propped her legs up resting her chin on her knees.

"Yeah I got 'em good this time." Beth said. "That'll teach 'em not to call us names." Setting the lantern on the ground Beth sat down next to Sarah.

"OK Sarah what's this exciting news you wanted to tell me about?" Beth asked.

"Well where to start." Sarah said. "My Uncle George came to see us a few days ago. He and Granny had not seen each other for about twenty years. They did a lot of catching up. Then he shared a song with us that he had written. I'll sing it for you later. Anyway he wants to take me on a road trip to sing on the radio for a friend of his. I'll be gone all summer. Granny prayed about it and she had a dream and the Lord let her know it was OK for me to go."

Beth sat quietly and listened which was unusual for her. As Sarah finished the story Beth put her arms around her and kissed her on the cheek.

"Sarah, I'm so proud of you. Your voice is unique, no one can sing like you. I think it's going to take you on lots of journeys. I'm gonna miss you though." Beth said trying to hold back a tear.

"This is what I was thinking Beth." Sarah said. "Do you think that your mom would let you come with me?"
Beth looked at Sarah. "Are you kidding? You really want me to go with you?" Beth perked up.

"Yes Beth, I think we would have a swell time and I'm sure Uncle George wouldn't mind." Sarah said thinking it all through.

Beth, full of excitement stood for a moment then with great exuberance she hugged Sarah and said, "Do you think mama will really let me go?"

"Well, that's why Granny wants to talk to her." Sarah said. They both looked hopeful.

"I can't wait for this afternoon to get here." Beth said. "I know, me too." said Sarah.

It's still early morning. Time seemed to drag on, and on, it was crawling at a snail's pace. Summer days were like that lazy, hot days almost as if time had stood still.

"Let's go back to the lake Sarah and see if the boys have left so we can go swimming. I can't wait for mama to talk to Granny.

Swimming will make the time go by faster." Beth said. Wishing. As if doing so, she could somehow speed up time.

Leaving the cool, dark cave and entering the bright sunshine, the girls squinted, adjusting their eyes to see.

"WOW it sure is hot out here, it must be 110 degrees. Uncle George said it's gona be a hot summer." Sarah said looking for some shade.

"Beth do you see them, have they gone?" Sarah asked rubbing her eyes and shielding them with her hands.

Beth put her hands to her eyes and said, "Yes, it looks like they have left the lake. Come on lets go. I can't take this heat anymore."

Sarah heard a splash. So she ran to the rope that was hanging from the tree, grabbed it swung out over the lake, and yelled, "Geronimo!" then dropped into the cool refreshing water.

Coming up out of the water she threw her head back and gave it a shake, she lay back on the water and began to float. Becoming one with the water she left the cares of the world behind and relaxed as she thought about nothing. The girls played and swam in the lake all afternoon.

"Come on Beth let's get out for a while, I'm getting hungry." Sarah splashed around a few more times.

"OK Sarah." Beth swam to the other side of the lake and climbed up on the bank. She laid back in the shade, threw her arms up over her head and stared at the clouds. Sarah followed.

"This really is the life isn't it Beth? No worries, no one to tell us what to do. Just lie here and enjoy the beauty all around us." A gentle breeze rustled through the trees as the girls watched the clouds being transformed into whimsical shapes and images. Serenity and peacefulness surrounded them as they were lost in their own thoughts. About that time they heard a noise. They both sat up leaning on their elbows and looked in the direction of the sound.

Both girls sat and stared. "Shh be real still Beth." Sarah whispered holding her breath, frozen in place.

"Tommy? Jimmy? Is that you?" Beth yelled.

Coming out of a bush was a skunk; they all saw each other at the same time. Startled the skunk began hissing and scratching. The girls wide eyed jumped up as fast as they could, then screamed and made a mad dash for the lake. As they did the skunk, also scared, let his spray fly…they were not fast enough, he hit his mark.

They came up out of the water gasping and coughing. Oh that horrible smell. Tears came to their eyes they could hardly breathe. They ran all the way home hacking and gaging.

"Pee U, Pee U" was all they could say in between gasps! There was an awful taste in their mouths their stomachs wretched, they broke out in a sweat, and then they threw up! They took off running towards home.

Tommy and Jimmy smelled them before they saw them.

"Lookie there Jimmy, a couple of polecats are heading this way. Run for the hills." Tommy said holding his nose.

Tommy and Jimmy ran, laughing the whole way as they watched the girls run.

Tommy yelled, "It serves you right Freckles and Lotto. Pew, you girls sure do stink!" The girls were mortified.

"Your new names are polecat number1 and polecat number 2. Pee U, ya'll will never get that stink out." The boys rolled with laughter and sweet revenge.

"Sarah! Stop right there!" Granny yelled as she smelled her running towards the house.

"Go out back I'll be there in a minute to de-skunk you." Granny grabbed a towel and held it over her nose she laughed and gaged at the same time.

Even Taffy, who always ran to greet Sarah, yelped and ran under the house to hide. Beth had the same welcome at her house.

Granny learned a long time ago that tomato juice does not work. She pulled her de-skunk recipe out of the cupboard and read.

- 1 quart 3% hydrogen peroxide
- ¼ cup baking soda
- 1 teaspoon liquid detergent

Mix in a large, open container and use immediately. Dilute with water afterwards and pour it down the drain. DO NOT STORE THE SOLUTION IT CAN EXPLODE.

To remove the smell from the house:

Boil vinegar in a pan, the house will smell like vinegar but after it goes away this will remove lingering skunk smells.

"Sarah I think we'll have to postpone your visit with your Dad's family due to these unusual circumstances. You'll have to wait until after you return from your trip," Granny said needing a bath herself.

"That does sound like a better idea Granny, I wouldn't want anyone to see, ah, smell me like this." Sarah said humiliated and down cast.

"Not only do I smell like a skunk, said Sarah, I smell like a veggie skunk!" Tears ran down Sarah's face from the vinegar.

On the Road

For a thousand years in thy sight are but as yesterday when it is past, and as a watch in the night. Psalm 90:4

George had finally made all the arrangements. Delayed a week, because of the skunk attack, they were now on their way. Beth's mom had agreed to let her go with Sarah. They were excited about the trip and had fully recovered from the ordeal with Mr. Skunk. Tommy and Jimmy would never let them live it down though. They could still hear them saying, "What goes around, comes around." The boys echoed each other, torturing the girls through the week.

Today was the day they would leave for Tennessee no more taunting from the boys and no more Mr. Skunk.

Granny packed some sandwiches and made jars of tea to take with them. George wasn't rich but after selling his land he was comfortable and would make sure the girl's needs were met. The hotel expenses would be paid for by the radio station and George would take care of the rest. George knew two things. One was that Sarah had talent, and two; he knew God was leading them.

40

After about an hour of being on the road the girls began to sing. The girl's voices were a perfect blend of harmony. Tears came to Uncle George's eyes.

"That was beautiful girls. I think that one will be added to your repo tour." Uncle George said listening as he drove down the highway.

Beth had a strong and mellow alto voice and wasn't shy in the least.

"Beth, would you be willing to sing that song with Sarah on the radio?" Uncle George asked?

"I sure would Uncle George. Sarah and I have been singing together for years. Where will we be singing first?" Beth asked with a glimmer in her eyes.

"Well we'll check into the hotel, get a bite to eat then see Mr. Berry. He'll have the sound room all set up for you. Now how 'bout another song?" Uncle George asked with expectation. The girls in unison began singing again.

"I come to the garden alone…while the dew is still on the roses…

Uncle George took a deep breath and said, "Girls there are no words to describe the peace and joy you have given an old man. If I never hear another song again I can leave this world in peace with the memory of your singing; *I Come to The Garden Alone,* and know I've been to heaven and back in those beautiful words and melody. I have a problem…I can't decide which song I want Mr. Berry to hear first, they are all perfect in every way."

Sarah looked at Uncle George. "Well then it really doesn't matter which one you choose now does it?" Sarah had a simple perspective that made perfect sense. As George pulled into a gas station they all laughed.

"Girls, while the attendant pumps the gas we better take a potty break it's another thirty miles to the next station." Uncle George said. "I'll grab us a coke cola and some snacks for the road."

"Filler-up." George said to the attendant. Reading his name tag. "Joe, make sure you check under the hood and give the windows a nice swipe if you don't mind?" George gave Joe a nod then headed towards the men's room.

"You got it mister." Joe nodded back and gave Sarah an odd glance but didn't say anything.

"Uncle George we'll meet you back here in about 15 minutes." Beth said.

Sarah and Beth went to get the bathroom key but as they stepped inside the front door the man behind the counter gave them a stern look, pursing his lips and looking like a Grinch, pointed to the sign on the wall. It read. "KEEP OUT-WHITES ONLY!!!"

Beth gasped. Sarah stepped back out the door feeling a little frightened and rejected but she was used to that.

Beth looked at the cashier eyes flashing with fire, said, "You should be ashamed of yourself we don't need your girls room anyway. It's probably got cooties!"

42

The man glared at Beth. Beth went out the door, put her arm around Sarah and said, "Come on Sarah I'm gonna tell Uncle George not to buy anything from this place except the gas."

As the girls got back into the car Beth told Uncle George what happened. Uncle George paid the attendant then they left.

Driving away they were quiet and in their own thoughts, George spoke first.

"I'm sorry girls we'll probably see a lot of prejudice along the way. Remember who you are in the Lord and let his love and wisdom guide you. You handled that pretty good back there. Hopefully things will change one day. Only the love of God can overcome this kind of hate. Stick together though and don't let it get you down." Said Uncle George wishing he could take the hurt away.

Sarah still shaking let out a slow gentle sigh and said, "I guess I've been holding my breath the whole time. Every time something like this happens I pray silently that God will protect me and that His Spirit will change their hearts towards my people. The colored side and the white side I really don't know why there has to be a side. I'm used to being in the middle. If not for the Lord I don't think I could take it. Granny always says, "Turn the other cheek like Jesus did." But sometimes I want to scream at people."

Beth took Sarah's hand and held it to her chest. "Well if anyone thinks they're going to hurt my friend they have another think coming." said Beth.

Beth is very bold and speaks her mind. That red hair is a fair warning to all, to beware.

43

They drove about two miles down the road, and came to a little Mom and Pop café, with a neon sign that read, *"Paradise."*

"Girls wait here let me go check it out." George said pulling into the parking lot.

The elderly lady that met him at the door was mulatto. She wore a scarf tied around her head and large hoop earrings hung on each ear. When she smiled a gold tooth glistened almost as much as her dark eyes.

She spoke with a strange accent one George was not familiar with.

"Com in Mon all is welcome here, com in welcome to Paradise." The jovial lady said.

George smiled and thought. "There's nothing to fear here."

He waved his hand for the girls to come on in.

"Yes girls, com in. Do not be frightened here com sit by deh window. I am Zeema. I am from deh Bahamas. Com sit. Tell Zeema what you like."

George and the girls looked at each other and then walked to the table Zeema pointed to and sat down.

The room was colorful, bright and very festive. Calypso music played in the background. A center piece with coconuts, pineapples and fresh flowers were on each table. Little plastic parrots hung from the ceiling and a live parrot of green, yellow and red was perched cage less, in one corner of the room.

"Morn'n Mon! Morn'n Mon! Rawww" The colorful bird screeched.

As they sat down Zeema handed them a tiny menu, she was smiling the whole time.

"Little missy's what can Zeema get you?" Zeema asked.

Sarah and Beth's eyes got real wide. They looked over the menu. There were peanut butter and banana sandwiches. Pineapple Boats filled with chicken salad made with grapes and walnuts, Tuna salad on Hawaiian bread, A Specialty punch and a fruit dish with cantaloupe, watermelon, Brazil nuts, pineapple and kiwi. For desserts there was key lime pie or a coconut chocolate chip cookie the size of a small saucer.

George seeing their expressions said. "We'll have some sweet ice tea, a tuna sandwich and the fruit salad for each of us."

"Okay mon." Zeema said then walked over to the other side of the counter and began preparing their food.

"Uncle George I've never seen anything like this. There's so much life and energy, it's a place of happiness. Don't you think so too Sarah?" Beth said looking around in awe.

Sarah agreed, she was mesmerized by everything especially Zeema.

Uncle George chuckled and said, "Well it is quite unique."

Sarah walked over to the bird; a sign was hanging from the birds perch that read. "My name is Smilie."

Sarah looked at the bird and said, "Good morning Smilie it's nice to meet you. My name is Sarah."

Smilie side stepped along the wooden dowel he perched on and moved his head from side to side.

"Morn'n Mon! Morn'n Mon." The parrot screeched in his parrot voice. Sarah laughed.

Zeema looked over at them and said, "Smilie like you, little miss. Sarah means princess. You are royalty. I can see it in you."

Sarah looked at Zeema questioningly. "No I'm not royalty. I'm Sarah from Alabama."

"Oh no miss, you are from royal blood and you have a very special gift. Isn't this true?"

"Well, yes I do have a special gift I sing and play music. And I'm a Christian." Sarah said.

"Then there you go royal blood. Jesus is the King of All. And you are one of his princesses. Are you not?" Zeema asked. It was more of a statement than a question.

"Yes I guess you are right I never thought of it that way before. My Granny told me my name means princess." Sarah was beaming and asked, "But how did you know, Zeema"

"I also have a gift. I see tings about others. And I too am of royal blood. I come from a faraway place and am here for a special purpose. I discover dis when I was a child. We, you and I are marked for a beautiful plan. You see our skin it is not brown and it is not white. It is blended specially by our King. He chose us for some ting different. There are no coincidences in His Kingdom. He does tings for a very specific reason. You have a long life ahead of you. You will journey to many places and sing for many people. Do not be discouraged and do not let disappointments keep you down. Always remember Zeema tell you dis day. You are here for a very special purpose. Now, Sarah, sing for me."

Sarah without hesitation lifted her voice and sang with all her heart.

"O Lord my God…When I in awesome wonder, consider all, the world's thy hands have made…." She sang with feeling and power.

Everything got real quiet and still, as she sang the beautiful hymn. The bird didn't stir. Zeema listened with eyes closed, tears streaming down her face the brightness of God shinning all over her as she rocked back and forth to the music.

Sarah's voice was clear and sweet full of power and passion. When she finished singing Zeema grabbed her and hugged her real tight.

"Oh my child I was right you are indeed very special. Never let no one rob you of dis gift. Guard yourself and keep your heart pure and good tings will come to you. There is a strong anointing on your life." Zeema said. "Now I must feed you before you all faint from hunger." Zeema worked on getting their lunch order ready.

Sarah went back to the table. Uncle George and Beth smiled and said. "You see Sarah you are, very special."

"Well you are very special too Beth. Sarah said. "And you too Uncle George." As she sat down and put her napkin in her lap.

Zeema served them their meal and gave them fruit punch instead of tea, made from an original recipe that has been in her family for generations. It included coconut milk, pineapple juice, cherries, mango and her secret ingredient, which was a bit of rum to add a little spice.

"Zeema, would you mind telling us how you came to be in these parts?" George asked as he took a sip of his punch. "Um this is good." He said taking another drink.

"Of course, Zeema, be happy to tell you." She said as she sat down at the table and began her story. "I was born in de Bahama's. I had four sisters and five brothers. I was the baby of de bunch. I am now 70 years old. As you can see I have been here a long time." Zeema said as she stretched her arms out hands face up, she spread them wide and presented herself to them.

They all looked at her with surprised looks on their faces and said, "You sure don't look seventy years old." They spoke at the same time and then burst into laughter.

There were no wrinkles in her face. Her skin was clean, without blemishes it was a soft mocha color. But what made her look even younger was the brightness in her eyes and face when she smiled. You could feel the love radiating from her. The magnetism of her accent and pleasant disposition made you want to stay and listen to her all day.

"Thank you." Zeema said. "But I assure you it be deh truth. When I was about your age, ten are you not little misses?"

She didn't wait for them to answer. "My Ma'mah died. So my Pa'pah decided to bring us to A-mer-ree-ca. We worked very hard and soon had enough money to bring us to dis country. It was 1896. We moved from place to place trying to find a home. People back din did not care for people like us. It is pretty much deh same today because our skin was different and we talked strange to dim. Finally we settled here. I've been here for twenty years. My brothers and sisters were spread throughout the U.S. only three are living. My Pa'pah died shortly after coming here. But tings got better after I moved here."

Zeema became a little teary eyed as she continued she said. "I made a living giving piano and dancing lessons, as well as, voice. I had a natural talent for deh music and made a good living. I opened dis place to serve Jesus. And have helped many along their way." Zeema looked around the café as she spoke.

"When deh good Lord tells you to do someting you have to do it. Zeema picked up a piece of pineapple and popped it into her mouth savoring the sweet morsel then swallowed. She then said. "There is such a blessing when you obey deh Lord. Do whatever He says to do. Do it in faith even if it seems foolish or unbelievable and he turns it into believable. God is pleased when we obey Him."

Turning to Uncle George she said. "We have His word to teach us and we have His Spirit to lead us. What more can we ask for? When we have Him we have everyting." She smiled and turned to look at Sarah and Beth. The girls returned the smile.

"Once there was a woman who was with child. She had no family to help her she come to Zeema for help. She said Jesus told her to come to me. I feed her and give her place to rest. Then the little one was born and he was very small. But he lived. Our Savior smiled on us he is now a doctor in Africa. I have many stories I could tell you but there is no time now. I do what the good Lord tells me to do and he blesses." Zeema smiled, closed her eyes, threw a kiss towards heaven and said, "Bless you my King of glory."

"Zeema, that is an amazing story," George said. "You are a very wise woman. Thanks for sharing your life with us. You are absolutely right about Jesus, he is everything we need. As a matter of fact we are on our way right now to Nashville. God has sent us on a mission. Sarah will be singing on the radio, a song that the angels gave me. Beth will be singing with her as well."

"Dis be very good." Zeema said. "I must know deh time and radio station so Zeema can listen." She said.

"Give me your phone number." Uncle George said, "And I will call you."

"Yes, yes that is good idea." Zeema said as she went to the counter to write her name and phone number down then handed it to George.

"Sarah," Zeema said, "When you sing, draw each breath from your diaphragm and sing with all your heart and soul. Your voice is very strong. It will touch the people in their hearts. Sing with confidence and purpose. You will do very, very well. It is for the glory and praise of Jesus. Zeema will be listening to you Miss

Sarah and Miss Beth." As Zeema spoke she reached out and patted Sarah's diaphragm letting her know what she meant.

Zeema gave each of them a hug and said. "I bless you in the name of deh great King and Savior Jesus. Bless you on your journey and may peace and mercy go with you." Then she said, "I have packed you some cookies made with coconut and walnuts and some of my famous punch. Remember Zeema. Call me. I will be patiently waiting."

The girls hugged Zeema, thanked her for everything and then went over to say good-bye to Smiley.

"Bye miss! Bye miss! Rawww was Smiley's reply.

As they drove away Zeema waved and whispered a prayer that God would protect and provide for them.

The clouds grew dark and lightning flashed as they made their way down the road.

"Storms coming." George said.

Before long it was pouring down rain. The wipers swished back and forth not helping much. George had to pull off the road it was impossible to see where he was going.

"Girls we need to pray that this storm passes soon and that no one runs into us while we are sitting here." George said whispering a prayer under his breath; he didn't want to frighten the girls.

An hour passed before the rain finally let up. It was about 2:30 in the afternoon. Uncle George started the car and they were on their way again.

As he pulled out onto the highway Beth said. "Look at that beautiful rainbow."

"No, there are two." Sarah said. "Do you see them?"

"Yes I do." Beth said astonished at the sight.

"It's a double rainbow!" The girls said simultaneously as they drew in their breath and then laughed. Each color was distinct from the other. There was yellow, blue, orange, green and lavender. Sarah grabbed her camera and took a picture.

George glanced at it as he drove, then went on. He said. "Girls this is a good sign. The Lord is letting us know He is with us and reminding us of His promise that He would never flood the earth again." George sat there grinning and thinking about the goodness of God.

Then Sarah began to sing, "Somewhere over the rainbow way up high….Beth joined in. There's a land that I heard of once in a lullaby…

Driving along George listened to the song and God began to speak to his spirit. *"My promises are yea and amen. I will never leave you nor forsake you. I will be with you to the end."* Tears came to George's eyes; he felt a resolve. He knew he was in God's perfect will.

At five o'clock that evening they came to a hotel in Shelbyville, Tennessee and decided to stop for dinner. The place was clean, there didn't seem to be an issue with what color a person was. George, Sarah and Beth went to the dining room. The hostess seated them. They ordered and ate in silence each one was content to be in their own little world. Afterwards they washed up and were back on the road again.

Sarah and Beth yawned, laid their heads against their window and dozed off. George drove until about ten o'clock he started getting sleepy so the next hotel he came to he pulled in and stopped. "Girls," George said. "Wake up we'll be staying here tonight."

The next morning they got up early, went to the dining room for breakfast and talked about their trip.

"Uncle George, do you really think we'll have a chance of getting on the radio?" Sarah asked in anticipation.

"Oh yes, honey I do." Uncle George said. "Even if Mr. Berry wasn't a good friend of mine your voice alone would win him over. Don't you worry everything is going according to plan."

Beth yawned and kept eating her oatmeal and toast.

"Beth, are you awake?" Sarah asked laughing at her friend.

Beth usually high spirited in the morning, well, she's high spirited all the time, said, "Sarah, I had a weird dream last night. We were on a little boat and we were fishing. But there were no fish. The fish were floating on top of the water dead." Then I heard you say. "Beth, get the net and collect the fish." I put the net in the water and all of a sudden fish started jumping in the boat. It was like the story where Jesus told Peter to cast his net on the other side, and the net was filled to over flowing. Then I woke up. I couldn't get back to sleep for a long time. I guess that's why I'm so sleepy. What do you think it means?"

Uncle George looking at Beth said, "There is a strong calling on your life, Beth. I believe God is letting you know you will be a fisher of men, well, and of women" He laughed. "But seriously you should think about going to Bible College and pursue the call God has on your life."

"That's the second time someone has said that to me." Beth said.

She thought about what he said for a few minutes' and said, "How would I go about it?"

George looked at Beth and seeing she was serious said, "Well you still have a few years before you can get started but you'll be ahead of the game if you inquire about it now. I'll get you some information as soon as we get back home. But remind me, OK?"

"That's sounds great Uncle George. Daddy tells me all the time to think about what I want to do with my life when I grow up. And for as long as I can remember I've wanted to tell others about the goodness of God. It's always on my mind." Beth said as she reached for a cookie.

George looked at his watch. "Girls we are making real good time. We should be in Nashville by dinner time."

Beth and Sarah were looking over some songs discussing which ones they should sing.

"Do you want to do our version of Amazing Grace, Beth?" Sarah asked

"Yeah and what about the Garden song we do that one really good?" Beth said as she turned several pages of the song book.

"That sounds swell Beth." Sarah said. "How many songs are we supposed to do Uncle George?"

"I'm not real sure," said George. "But have two lined up in case Mr. Berry wants to hear more after you do the Angel song."

"Sarah you never did get to sing the Angel song for me. Will you sing it now?" Beth asked as she closed the song book and set it aside.

Sarah placed the song book on the seat next to her and began to sing in her soprano voice. Her range was amazing. Beautiful sweet soprano notes came from Sarah's voice. She sang with purpose and passion. The way she sang lifted you into another dimension lost in the beauty of the sound and the words of the angel song.

Though times are hard
I'm by your side
Your tears I hold within my hand
No matter what I'll hold you close
Look to the one who understands.

Though fears may come and tears may fall
Be still and know that I am God
Let perfect peace restore your heart
And know my love we'll never part

Chorus:
I walked the road of trials and torment

I sat with those who love me still

But on the cross

I felt the suffering of all the ones who loved me most.

The birds they sing a nightly chorus

Of joy and peace to all they bring

So lift your voice and head toward heaven

And learn their song, their song and sing.

He gives me peace, He gives me life, the angels sing be glorified

Praise to the King our mighty King

We're going home on angels wings.

When in the stillness now at midnight

I see the star of love so bright

I'll never ever doubt my Savior

For he will lead me through the night

And on the breeze I hear Him whisper...

Press on my child and do not weep

For at the dawn you'll have your answer

So close your eyes and go to sleep.

Chorus:

I walked the road of trials and torment

I sat with those who love me still

But on the cross

I felt the suffering of all the ones who loved me most.

The birds they sing a nightly chorus

Of joy and peace to all they bring

So lift your voice and head toward heaven

And learn their song, their song and sing.

He gives me peace, He gives me life,

The angels sing be glorified

Praise to the King our mighty King

We're going home on angels wings.

Beth took a breath and with tears streaming down her face all she could do was weep.

Finally she said, "Sarah that is the most beautiful song I've ever heard. I might only be ten years old but I can feel God's Precious Spirit in that song. When you sing that song everyone who hears it will be truly blessed. It's like God comes and sits right inside your heart and loves you and knows exactly what you've been through." Beth wiped her eyes, took a deep breath and thought, "Lord Jesus I want to make you happy with my life by helping others know you."

"I know Beth it touches my heart too." Sarah said. "God knew what Uncle George was going through when he gave him the song. It was truly a gift from the angels." Then Sarah reached out and patted Beth's hand.

Uncle George was crying too and said, "It was given to me Sarah, so I could share it with others, but I needed someone who could truly do it justice that's why I came to see you." Uncle George said. "God knew who he wanted to sing it I'm so proud it was you.

That song is the reason we are going to Nashville. Through the radio we'll be able to reach even more people." He said as he looked back at his amazing niece and her best friend.

"I just want to glorify the Lord Uncle George." Sarah said. "And if he wants to use me to do that I am willing. I want to be pleasing to the Lord more than anything."

"I know you are Sarah and that makes it even better that He chose you. Your humble and sweet spirit makes all the difference in the world. Especially since I know the heartache you've had to face." George spoke with compassion and tenderness in his voice.

"Thanks Uncle George." Sarah said as tears filled her eyes. "That means a lot to me."

Beth spoke up. "As long as I've known Sarah, and that's been my whole life, she's always been humble and sweet. Even when the kids make fun of her and call her names she stays calm. I don't understand how people can be so cruel." Beth said as she sat up straighter in her seat.

"I don't understand it either." Sarah said thinking back. "This one day at school I was all alone in the girl's restroom. A boy came in behind me and poked me with a stick. I couldn't see who he was; he grabbed my hair and shoved me against the wall and held me there. He said, "Half breed if you tell anyone about this I'll kill your dog." Then he spit on the back of my head." Sarah was trembling.

Beth shocked and stunned said, "SARAH…you never told me that."

"I was too frightened Beth." Sarah said remembering the terror; a shiver ran up her back.

"When did that happen?" Beth asked staring straight into Sarah's eyes noticing the hurt and fear as she looked at her dearest friend.

"It was last year. I still can't go to the girl's bathroom by myself. I always make sure there is someone else around me when I go." Sarah had a distant look on her face thinking back.

"Sarah, this is serious you need to go to the principal about it so he can notify the authorities." George said with great concern in his voice.

"It won't do any good. They won't listen to a ….well you know." Sarah began to cry. Beth put her arm around her and tried to console her.

"Don't worry Sarah everything is going to change." Uncle George said. "I'll see to it. Don't cry sweetheart. We'll get through this." George was furious and would not rest until he put an end to this harassment. "We'll get to the bottom of this I promise."

Beth was angry too. "Yeah and I'll be by your side like glue from now on. No one's gonna hurt my Sarah. Oh this makes me mad." Beth said her face red as she clenched her teeth.

All of a sudden they heard a big bang, it sounded like a gun went off. The car swerved, George had a hard time keeping the car on the road. The car was facing the opposite direction as they spun around and came to a stop. Thankfully no other cars were around.

"Girls are you alright?" Exasperated, George sat for a moment trying to catch his breath.

59

"Yes we're OK." They said as they checked each other out to make sure. Shaken a little but not hurt.

"Girls this is what I want you to do." Uncle George said as he looked one way then the other making sure no cars were coming.

"I want you to go stand by that dogwood tree. We've had a blowout." Getting out of the car and assessing the situation. "Yep, I can see the nail."

The girls did as Uncle George said. Then he got back in the car and slowly turning the car in the right direction he drove the car off the road. He got out of the car, rolled his sleeves up and opened the trunk to take out the jack and spare tire. Beth and Sarah then walked over to where Uncle George was beginning to work. He started to jack the car up when a tow truck pulled up behind him. Two ladies who were probably in their early thirties got out of their truck and said, "Howdy mister, looks like you could use a hand. I'm Molly and this here is my twin sister Holly. We own a garage up the road a piece."

Molly and Holly wore overalls. They had short brown hair that poked out of their cap that read M&H Garage. Both women bent over and spit right at the moment George said hello. They wiped their mouth with their hand and said, "Looks like ya'll need a new tar we can help if'n you won't us too."

George, Sarah and Beth just stared. Sarah and Beth looked at the ground where a stream of brown spittle plastered the dirt. The smell of the snuff rose to their nasal passages causing them to almost gag. Taking a step back they gawked at the two ah, women.

Rubbing his nose George said. "Well, ah, yes I think I could use a hand. My spare is flat too. You came along just in time."

Sarah and Beth stood like two statues, frozen and immovable. Molly and Holly paid no attention to their responses.

Molly said, "I'll hook your car up to my truck and we'll tow it up the road a piece. If that's OK with ya'll?"

"Sure." George said as he scratched his head in bewilderment and thought to himself, "they look harmless enough."

Holly looked at the girls who were still staring at the dirt. Then she said, "We ain't got fer to go ya'll get in your car and we'll give ya a tow."

Sarah and Beth turned like two mechanical robots and got into their car still mesmerized by the situation. They sat very still all the way to the garage.

Pulling into the yard where an old garage stood, there were rusty, old tireless cars scattered around the place. They were discarded old junk no use to anyone. Five skinny dogs lifted their heads as Holly and Molly pulled into the un-kept yard. When the dogs saw Sarah and Beth get out of the car they came over to them, sniffed them, not very interested then went and laid back down in the dirt. All except for one, it was a Chihuahua. He yapped non-stop.

"Hush up Tater." Holly scolded. She bent down and scooped the dog up and began scratching his head.

"We call em Tater, cause he's no bigger than a tater. He's always yapping about something. Ain't that right Tater?" Holly said. Tater gave a little yelp enjoying getting his ears scratched.

"Its OK girls they won't bite come on in, Molly will fix the tar in no time. While she's do'n that I'll get Maw ta fix ya'll some lunch. It's not much but it'll fill the Ole gizzard." Holly said.

George looking a little baffled said, "Oh no that's alright we don't want to put you to any bother."

"Naw bother a'tall we got plenty. Maw's in the house she's been cooking all morn'n. We always feed the folks when they come through here." Molly said.

"Maw, we got comp'ney." Holly shouted from the yard.

Maw came to the screen door. She was short in stature with an apple shape to her body about 55 years old. She had round rim glasses perched on the tip of her nose. Graying hair pulled tight from her face was twisted into a bun at the back of her head. Her face was flushed from rushing to see who was there.

"Ya'll come in I'll fix ya some iced tea. I've got fried chicken, collard greens, fried taters and corn bread. And I fixed some of my famous nanner pudd'n.

Beth and Sarah's stomach was growling. They came alive and both spoke up. "That sounds swell." said Sarah. "Yeah I'm real hungry." Beth said holding her stomach.

"Is it OK Uncle George?" The girls asked.

George grinned. "I guess so. I love southern hospitality. It's been a long time since I've had banana pudd'n." He let out a little laugh and said, "Thanks ma'am."

"Come on in and make yourself at home." Maw said as she opened the screen door.

As Sarah got closer, Maw saw she was mulatto. She didn't say a word didn't even blink an eye. Entering the house they saw a baby sleeping in a play pen. To their surprise the baby was also mulatto.

"This here is Mandy short for Amanda. She's my pride and joy she's my great grand-baby. Molly is her maw. She got drunk one night and nine months later little Mandy was born. We wouldn't take a wooden nickel for her. So you come right on in here missy no one will snub you here." Maw said motioning for them to come in.

"Thank you ma'am I appreciate that." Sarah said as she smiled at the baby then noticed a piano in the corner of the room.

Maw caught her eyeing the piano. "Do you play missy?"

"Yes ma'am, I do. Would you like to hear a song?" Sarah said with no amount of shyness when it came to music.

"Yes, child I sure would." Maw took a jar out of her pocket and spit in it wiping her mouth with a red bandana afterwards. She tucked them both back into her pocket, sat down in her rocker and waited for Sarah to begin.

Sarah walked over to the piano, sat down, and began to play, singing softly.

"Just as I am without one plea but that thy blood was shed for me and that thou bidst me come to thee, oh Lamb of God I come…I come."

When Sarah had finished the song she looked at Maw, she was crying, rocking back and forth her hands folded in her lap.

"Oh child, I haven't heard that song in many a year." Maw said. "That was beautiful. You should be on the radio with talent like that. It sure would touch a lot of folk's hearts." Maw said wiping her eyes.

"Thank you Ma'am that's where we're headed. We're going to Nashville. We have an appointment tomorrow afternoon." Sarah said.

"Well you need to let us know when, because we'd love to hear ya." Maw said. "Molly has a phone in the garage. I'll get you the number before you leave."

"Yes ma'am we'll be sure to let you know." said Sarah.

Molly and Holly came in the house. "The tar's fixed, you're as good as new, mister." said Molly. "It had a big ole nail in it but we plugged it real good."

"Please call me George and this is Sarah and Beth my nieces." George said, he also claims Beth as his niece.

Both ladies nodded and said in unison, "Nice to meet ch'all."

"This here is Maw, and Mandy." Holly said.

"Yes we've been entertaining your Maw." George said as he cleared his throat.

Molly spoke up kinda loud, "I hear'd the music. That is a beautiful song. Yer voice is like an angel didn't even wake the baby."

Sarah stood up to walk away from the piano and said, "Thank you."

"The food is on the table ya'll go sit down and help yer selves. I'll get ya some tea. Maw said as she made her way to the kitchen. A yellow table cloth covered the round table where bowls of food sat in the middle. White dishes trimmed with tiny pink roses were placed where each person would sit. Maw brought mason jars of sweet tea and lemon from the kitchen for everyone. Then she said, "Help yer'self to the mustard."

Sarah looked at Uncle George as if to say, "We need to say grace." George and the girls held hands and said, "Would you mind if we say grace first?"

"By all means of course say grace." Maw said. They bowed their heads as George prayed.

"This is delicious Maw." Sarah said. "May I have a little more?"

Then Beth added. "Yes very delicious. Thank you for all your trouble."

"Weren't no trouble a-tall." Maw said. "And help yourself eat as much as you want we got plenty."

As they were finishing lunch Mandy began to stir. She turned over, lifted her head and made a little whimper.

Molly jumped up to get her. She picked Mandy up off of the pallet and kissed her all over her neck and face. Mandy giggled and held onto her mother's face.

"How old is she?" Beth asked.

"She's 9 months old. She ain't no bigger than a minute. She got her curls from her daddy but I ain't seen him since, well since that night, just as well him being a Negro and all. But Mandy is as healthy as anything. She's a little but plump but babies should be plump. She laughs all the time, she's happy, and that's all that matters. I couldn't ask for a baby no-better." Molly said as she sat in the rocker and fed Mandy. "And she eats like a little pig."

They all laughed.

'Miss Sarah, would you mind playing us another song?" Holly asked as she sat down on the couch.

"Not at all come on Beth let's do the one the angels gave to Uncle George." Sarah said as she motioned for Beth to come over to the piano.

When the girls had finished the song there was not a dry eye in the house.

Even lil Mandy had a tear roll down her cheek.

"Girls, we've been here for thirty years, Maw's been here fifty years and no one has ever sang for us like that. Even the preacher neglects to come see us. I guess us having a part white, part colored baby keeps folks away. We do the best we can here. Never hurt anybody. Helping anyone who needed a hand and thankful to do it. Ya'll are the first folks whoever did anything for us. And we'll never forget it. Holly said as she dried her eyes.

"This Jesus you speak of, can anyone meet him? Or is he just for special folks?" Maw said and was very serious. She wanted this Jesus to live in her heart. "When I was a little-un I heard people sing like that first song you did. But I never knew what it was all about." Maw said wiping her eyes and blowing her nose.

George looked at Molly then Holly, then at Maw and Mandy. He could not believe what he was hearing.

"Ladies, Jesus is for who-so-ever-will!!! John 3:16 says. *For God so loved the world that he gave his only begotten son that who-so-ever believeth in him should not perish but have ever lasting life. Verse 17: For God came not into the world to condemn the world but that the world through him might be saved."* George said.

"Mister George, I want this Jesus. I want him to come into my heart." Molly said.

"Me too." said Holly.

"Yes, and me too," Maw said as tears ran down her cheeks.

They all held hands and bowed their heads.

George looked up at them with love and compassion and said, "Repeat after me."

"Lord Jesus come into my heart forgive me of all my sins. I believe you are the son of God. I believe you died for me and rose again. I accept you as my Savior. I want to live for you, I want to serve you. I want to tell others about your great love. Thank you Jesus for saving me amen!"

After they prayed Molly spoke up. "I feel as light as a feather. I don't even want any tobacco and I always want it after I eat."

"I've tried for years to break the habit, now I feel like a brand new person; light and free." Molly said.

"Me too," said Holly.

"Oh my Lord, I just saw a vision of Jesus. He appeared right before my eyes just now. Maw said.

"Matilda Rose how do you expect me to heal you if you keep putting that snuff in your system?" Jesus said.

"I was shocked!" said Maw. "Imagine Jesus the son of the almighty talking to me?"

Then he said, "Throw it away!" and he vanished.

Maw stood up; looked at everyone; took the jar out of her apron along with the snuff and ran outside. She poured the snuff over a red ant bed and watched as it killed every one of the ants.

"If it does that to ants imagine what it does to the body?" Maw thought and then said. "Thank you Jesus, I'll never touch the stuff ever again!"

Maw came back inside and everyone was rejoicing and praising the Lord!

Sarah went to the piano and they began to sing. *"Oh when the saints go marching in…Oh when the saints go marching in…*

Oh Lord I want to be in that number…when the saints go marching in."

Molly, Holly and Maw began marching around the house and shouting. "Praise the Lord we're saved!!!"

They fell on their knees, raised their hands and started speaking in a heavenly language. Revival had hit their souls. What rejoicing and celebration.

Sarah said, "Uncle George there's that funny language again…what is it?"

But before Uncle George could answer, Sarah was speaking in the funny language herself. Beth started laughing and couldn't stop. George slapped his hands and began praising God for the joy of the Lord and for the salvation of three new souls who had come to Jesus; faith simple and childlike. This is what he had been praying for.

"Holly go to the garage and get Cousin Billy Jo, he needs this too! Then go next door and tell Bertha, Jed and Ida-Mae to come over here. I want them to get in on this. And tell them to bring their instruments with them, and hurry!" Maw said.

"What's wrong Matilda Rose is the house on fire?" Billy Jo asked rushing into the house in a huff, ready to fight fire.

"Well in a way it is Billy Jo." Molly said laughing and crying at the same time.

"I heard shout'n over here, is everyone aw right?" Bertha said, wheezing trying to catch her breath.

Maw laughed and said, "Come on in here I want you to hear and see this for yourself. Girls sing that angel song again."

Soon the house was full of friends, and family. Sarah and Beth kept singing the angel song. People cried and fell on their knees and prayed to God to forgive them of their sins. As they did the Holy Ghost took over and everyone in the room began to sing and shout and dance and speak in a heavenly language. Sarah and Beth sang and God showed up in a mighty way. At midnight the glory of God was still moving.

Some shouted…

Some cried…

Some laughed…

Some danced…

Some spun around.

Cigarette packs were laid on the kitchen table…

Hurts and feuds that had gone on for years were forgiven…

Hearts were healed; people were delivered and set free….Soon everything quieted down; there was so much love in the place no one wanted to leave. George finally stood up and read from the bible.

"Acts 2:4 - And they were all filled with the Holy Spirit, and began to speak with other tongues, as the Spirit gave them utterance.

"You see, brothers and sisters what happened here tonight, is scriptural. So tomorrow when you wake up and wonder what happened here tonight take out your bibles and read from the book of Acts. Then find yourselves a spirit filled Church to attend on Sunday." George was full of the joy of the Lord.

They all clapped their hands and said, "Thank you Brother and thank you Sarah and Beth for coming our way."

It was one o'clock in the morning some people were still in God's presence. A few people started to make their way toward the door hugging and saying goodnight. "Maw we'll see you in Church, Sunday. Won't the preacher be surprised when we all show up?"

Maw agreed her heart was full as she looked around at some still lying on the floor praying and seeking God.

"What a mighty move of God. I've never seen nothing like this before." Maw said as she wiped tears from her eyes. Hearts were filled with joy and thankfulness.

George was speechless but had a smile on his face that could not be wiped away. He whispered a prayer.

"Thank you Jesus for showing up today let your spirit continue on in the lives of these people. Bless them; raise them up some prophets and ministers for this community let your word continue on here for your glory." Amen.

George and the girls slept til about 9:30 that morning. Maw cooked them a good breakfast. As they sat down to eat. Maw bowed her head and prayed.

"Lord, I've been far off for a long, long time. I even forgot about you. But you never forgot about me. I want to thank you for bringing these nice folks here. And for the Angel song that changed our lives. I won't let you down Lord and I'll never forget you again. Watch over Brother George, Sarah and Beth. Keep them safe on their journey. Bless their trip. And oh yea Lord, bless this food. Amen."

"That was a nice prayer Maw…God really loves you. He's been waiting for you a long time. He wants you to know you're a leader and he wants you to continue to bring his word to this community." George said taking a sip of his coffee.

"Oh George I don't know…"Maw said feeling inadequate.

But before she could finish…George held up his hand and said, "Don't be like Moses making excuses; God's given you Molly and Holly to help you. Read the bible to the people, sing songs to God and He'll show up and do the rest." George said seeing what Maw didn't quite get it yet.

"Well since you put it that way I guess we won't have a problem. I've got a lot to learn and I know now God is with me to lead and guide me all the way. Maw said with new faith and determination.

"You'll see Maw, you'll see." George picked up Maw's bible and said, "Read this book, pray in the Holy Ghost, and God will teach you all you need to know. He will send everything you need. Have faith in Jesus and trust Him." George gave Maw several scriptures to read and said, "One more thing, there's an enemy always on the lurk trying to destroy us. But Jesus will help you, call on His name draw close to Him and the enemy will flee."

"Alright George I'll do it." Maw said. "I'm a strong woman and with the good Lord on my side, we will win." George could see Maw was beginning to get hold of what he was saying.

After breakfast they all said their goodbyes. George and the girls left and were on the road again.

Everything was serene as they drove along the highway Sarah caught glimpses of dogwood trees most of their flowers gone. Maples and tall pines were thick with new growth the leaves a deep green for summer. Sarah was in deep thought; she looked to the sky and noticed an eagle flying high above the clouds. She saw it soar higher and higher until it was out of sight.

"What are you thinking about Sarah?" Beth asked following Sarah's gaze to some unseen object.

"Oh, I don't know I was thinking about how awesome it would be to fly and be able to see everything from heavens view." Sarah was thinking about her mom and dad.

"That would be something." Beth said as she pointed out an eagle's nest.

George said, "Look girls we're coming into the big city of Nashville." I think there's a new restaurant not far from here. They say they make the best hamburgers and shakes around. You girls want to get a bite to eat?" George could hear his stomach growling. He thought about Maws banana pudding and grinned to himself.

Then he whispered a prayer. *"Lord Jesus keep your hand on Maw and her family." Amen.*

The girls were giddy with excitement and yelled with glee. "Yes that sounds super!"

"Do you think we'll see anyone famous?" Beth asked.

"Who knows." said Uncle George. "There's no telling what will happen in this town." Uncle George laughed. "Girls, be ready for anything that's all I know to tell ya."

The Studio

Thou carriest them away as with a flood; they are as asleep: in the morning they are like grass which growth up. Psalm 90:5

Tipping the bellboy, Uncle George turned and said, "Girls I'll be right out I've got to make a phone call to the studio and then we'll be on our way. If you want to take a little break and freshen up I'll meet you in the lobby in ten minutes."

"That sounds great Uncle George. Sarah said. "We'll see you then." The girls didn't waste any time. After freshening up they were back out the door in a flash.

They spotted Uncle George he was reading a newspaper. He looked up, folded the paper and laid it on the table. He smiled and said, "Well you girls look real nice."

The girls smiled and said, "Thank you."

George said, "After you ladies." He held the door for them.

They headed to the car. Getting in the car Beth asked, "How long will it take to get to the studio?"

"About 5 minutes and we'll be there." Uncle George said as he pulled out of the parking space. The girls stared out of the car window, the wind blowing their hair back from their faces. They were excited and thrilled to finally be in Nashville.

The streets were crowded. Not like being in the country. The sights and the smells were completely different. Smelled like burnt rubber and stale air.

"Look how tall that building is." said Beth.

"And look at that one. And that one and Oh look at that one." Sarah said. Its big dome reminds me of pictures I've seen of medieval times." Sarah said, her eyes taking on the look of two round saucers spinning into oblivion, surveying street cars, sky and tall buildings, it was the city. Sights she'd never seen before.

"I can hardly wait to get to the studio." Sarah was twisting and turning, looking one way then the other. "Wait til Tommy and Jimmy hear about this. They'll be so jealous won't they Beth?" Sarah said showing her mischievous side. They were filled with exhilaration and anxiety as they drove along.

"I'm starting to get butterflies in my stomach, Beth, what about you?" Sarah asked as she rubbed her sweaty palms together.

"Yes I do feel a little light headed now that you mention it." Beth said and took a slow deep breath. She realized her heart was racing like a fox being chased by a hound.

"Breathe, Beth, just breathe." She said to herself.

"Wait until Mr. Berry hears you sing he's going to be thrilled. I can hardly wait for that." George said as he handed Sarah the map. "Tell me where we are and which way to turn to get to the studio." Uncle George said stopping at a red light. "That'll help take your mind off everything."

"OK, at the next street, turn to your right; it should be two blocks down on the left. There it is." Sarah pointed.

Parallel parking along the street was a bit of a challenge, but George did it perfectly. As they got out of the car Uncle George said, "Girls stay calm; you're going to be just fine."

"OK Uncle George if you say so." Beth said. Sarah nodded not knowing exactly what to expect.

"Stay close, the city is big and there's a lot going on." Uncle George said taking the girls hands leading them down the sidewalk.

"Oh my goodness this is much bigger than I pictured. The butterflies are really fluttering now," Sarah said. She squeezed Uncle George's hand tighter.

Beth was awe struck, her eyes got bigger and bigger. "At least we're walking downhill." Beth said.

"Come on girls you have nothing to be afraid of. They're gona love you." George said as he picked up the pace.

"Here it is Uncle George." Sarah stopped in front of the building, took a deep breath and said, "Here we go."

They walked to the elevator waited for the doors to open then stepped inside. George pushed the number four button. The girls felt their tummy's rise and fall as the elevator moved upwards. They giggled and said, "Oh my, that was fun!"

The doors opened and they stepped out into a lobby. The studio took up the whole fourth floor. Walking up to the receptionist desk where a lady was sitting and typing, they stood and waited. There was a name plate on her desk that said, Dana Jones.

"Hello, may I help you?" Miss Jones asked.

"My name is George Willis we have an appointment." George said straightening his tie.

"Yes Mr. Willis I know who you are. We've all been waiting for your arrival. Have a seat they'll be with you shortly." Miss Jones said as she buzzed Mr. Berry's office to let him know Mr. Willis and the girls had arrived.

Sarah and Beth sat down on a leather couch facing the elevator. Sarah got up and walked around the room.

"Beth come look at this." Sarah said as she pointed to a picture on the wall.

It was a picture of Elvis Presley and his new song *Heartbreak Hotel.* Along the wall was a gallery of pictures. Such as, Chet Atkins, Dolly Parton and Charlie Pride.

"This is so cool I can't believe it. We're in the very studio where Elvis recorded Heartbreak Hotel." Beth said as she scanned the wall of fame. "I saw this on television. I never dreamed I'd see this in person." Beth was elated and said, "Everyone at school will be pea green with envy."

Sarah looked at the picture of Charlie Pride and said, "Yes this is neat-O. She stared at Charlie Pride's picture. He's one of my hero's." Sarah said in amazement. "He's just like me, a mulatto."

Miss Jones came into the room then she said, "They're ready for you. Please follow me."

Sarah, Beth and George followed Miss Jones down a long hall-way. They entered a room where four men were sitting. There was Mr. Berry, Mr. Stevens, Mr. Atkins, and Mr. Roberts.

Mr. Berry greeted them with a hearty handshake and said, "I hear you girls can sing. Miss Jones is going to take you to the sound room and when you're ready she'll let us know. When you see the green light come on, we'll be able to hear you. When you're through a red light will come on and someone will be in to get you. OK? Are you ready?"

"You bet we are." Both girls replied.

"Come on girls follow me." Miss Jones was a petite lady about twenty-five years old. She had striking features, crystal blue eyes and auburn hair that just about touched her shoulders. Perfect straight white teeth you could tell she was genuine and sincere. You could see it in her eyes when she smiled.

"So girls is this your first time recording?" Miss Jones asked as she looked over her shoulder at the girls but kept walking.

Beth spoke up. "Yes it is. We're from Alabama we haven't been to the big city before." Feeling a little intimidated then she added, "But it's exciting."

"Oh, well maybe you'll get to see more of the city before you leave. What part of Alabama are you from?" Miss Jones stopped for a moment outside the door waiting for them to reply.

"A little town called Cedar Bluff." Sarah said as she blushed realizing she had spoken up.

Miss Jones ignored the blushing…but smiled and said, "I know exactly where that is I've been there many times on my way to Rome, Georgia. I've done some great fishing in Cedar Bluff at Weiss Lake on the Coosa River. It's the Crappie (fish) Capital of the world. Well, here we are.

"Yes you're right Miss Jones my Uncle George, Beth and I fish there often. Next time you come to town give us a call we'll go fishing with you," Sarah said. She was impressed with Miss Jones.

"You bet I will." said Miss Jones.

"Beth I'd like you to sit in this little room here and when it's time for your duet I'll come and get you. You'll be able to see Sarah through the window." Miss Jones motioned with her hand for Beth to have a seat.

"OK, swell." Beth said as she sat down and waited patiently for Miss Jones to get Sarah set up. The sound room was small. A microphone was hanging from the ceiling.

"You'll need to wear this head-set, watch for the green light to come on, count to five and then begin singing after it comes on. The first song you do will be a warm up. Then give us thumbs up when you're ready to begin your next song. Good luck." Miss Jones said as she turned to exit.

Sarah took the head-set placed it on her head and smiled at Miss Jones. The green light came on and Sarah sang a warm up song. All eyes were on her and all ears could not believe what they heard. Everyone started making notes. The musicians all smiled. The sound-man adjusted his keys. Mr. Berry stood in silence not giving away what he thought.

"Miss Sarah this will be the real thing this time. Are you ready?" The sound man said as Sarah gave him a thumbs up.

The green light came on. Sarah took a breath, closed her eyes, counted to five and began to sing *The Angel Song*.

When she finished everyone was crying. Sarah opened her eyes and stood very still waiting for the next cue. She had no idea the impact the song had made on everyone. She waited and waited and waited. All of a sudden the door flew open and all five men came rushing into the small room. Mr. Berry put his arm around Sarah and said, "Young lady in all the twenty-five years I've been doing this I have never…ever…heard anyone sing like you. The combination of your voice and the words of the song are astonishing."

"What do you mean Mr. Berry?" Sarah was a little astonished herself.

"It means dear child you're gonna be on the radio and we want to offer you a contract. I'm gonna want to hear more, but before we go any further I couldn't wait to congratulate you. Alright now let's all go back to the control room and hear a song with Sarah and Beth. I have a real good feeling about this." Mr. Berry said leading the way.

Sarah and Beth sang *Amazing Grace* in their special way which caused everyone to nod with enthusiasm. They all agreed that what they heard sealed the deal.

"Their voices blend beautifully. I want the director of RJO records, to meet them and hear the demo. This is going to be big and I do mean big. They have the talent and the looks; marketing is going to enjoy this. We'll also need media coverage. We'll need a story and pictures of these little ladies. This is going to sell. The possibilities are limitless." Mr. Berry said without taking a breath.

"George this is perfect, all we need is a contract and oh by the way, who is her legal guardian?" Mr. Berry said as he paced back and forth mind racing about all the ways he was going to promote Sarah and Beth.

George didn't know quite what to say. He stood there scratching his head. Then he said, "Her grandmother, Norma Jean. But I didn't know it would go so fast."

"Yes, yes we have to get her song out there. It'll affect millions. She's going to be a star. Where's Miss Jones?" Mr. Berry said rushing about.

Sarah looked at Beth then at her Uncle George. She was saddened by what she heard. George looked at her then at Beth then at Mr. Berry and back at Sarah.

"What is it George? What's wrong? Is there a problem?" Mr. Berry asked.

"I'm not sure how to tell you this." said George.

"What?" What's wrong?" Mr. Berry stood still and stared at George waiting for him to speak.

"Sarah doesn't want to sign a contract. She doesn't want to make a record if all its going to do is bring her fame." George said as he looked away a little embarrassed.

"WHAT!" Mr. Berry shouted. "I've never heard such nonsense." Mr. Berry was quite put out by this information.

Sarah spoke up. "Mr. Berry, Sir, you see it's like this. God has given me a special voice and talent for music but I cannot be so selfish to bring glory to myself. God is Holy and His music is Holy and it's to be shared with everyone so they can hear and come to know Him. You cried, sir. Didn't something happen in your heart? Didn't you want to know Him? This song is more than just a song. It touches the heart and it changes us somehow. He loves you, He died for you and He wants you to love Him too. I can't take money and fame when He wants to give people life and salvation. Won't you consider asking Him into your heart? I agreed to come and sing the song so people could know Him. God wants you to know Him, to love Him and follow Him. I may be young Mr. Berry but I know who God is and I feel His love inside me and around me. You see I'm not white and I'm not black, I'm a combination I guess, but it's not about the color of my skin. He loves me no matter what my color is, or who my parents were, and He wants everyone to know He loves them too and accepts them just the way they are. I know my voice will take me many places and it will touch many lives. I can't be boxed in by a contract Mr. Berry. I'm sorry if this upsets your plans but it's the way it has to be." Sarah never backed down when it came to talking about Jesus.

"When I was six years old I knew something was different about me. At school the other kids shied away from me. They'd laugh and talk behind my back. And call me bad names. That is everyone except for Beth. I didn't fit in with the black people and I couldn't fit in with the white's either. I didn't know where I belonged. One Sunday morning we were at Church. Granny always takes me to church and she'd sit with me on the back row. I started to notice that all the white kids would go to a special room but I had to stay with Granny. I asked Granny one day why my skin wasn't like other kids. And why my eyes were blue. And you want to know what she said? Sarah asked.

"What's that Miss Sarah?" Mr. Berry asked amazed at her candor and spunk. She had his full attention.

"My Granny said, "You have something they don't have, baby. You have the eyes of Jesus. But you need to ask Him to come into your heart to live there and to help you forgive when people hurt you. He was also talked about and rejected but He loved them anyway. Then you'll not only have His eyes, you'll have His heart too. So right there on that back row, my Granny and I prayed, and I asked Jesus to come live in my heart. From that day to this I've had a knowing; that no matter what happens in my life; Jesus will always be right by my side and living in my heart. Do you want Jesus to come live in your heart Mr. Berry?" Sarah asked, her blue eyes piercing his, she was dead serious.

Mr. Berry was flabbergasted, that's a word that means shocked. He'd never seen such boldness and wisdom come from someone so young.

Mr. Berry choked back tears. Holding his breath, palms sweaty, he looked Sarah straight in her brilliant blue eyes and said with a trembling voice, "Young lady in all my years I have never seen or heard such a message from one so young and talented. You have touched a part of my heart that has been closed up for a very long time. I've been running and spinning out of control and you just put a cog in my treadmill. I've lied and cheated and done very bad things in my life. When I heard you sing all I could think about was dollar signs but something else was happening as I listened, my stony heart was turning to mush. I didn't want to admit it though, that's why I was talking so fast. Hoping the feelings I was having would go away. You stopped me dead in my tracks. What do I do to receive this salvation you're talking about?" Tears pouring from his eyes, body trembling, Mr. Berry surrendered. Sarah took his hand.

"Uncle George; Beth; let's pray with Mr. Berry." Sarah took their hands and introduced Mr. Berry to Jesus.

"Jesus this is Mr. Berry; Mr. Berry this is Jesus." said Sarah.

"I've been waiting for you a long time Mr. Berry. Welcome to the family." Jesus smiled and gave Mr. Berry an extra blessing. Of course Mr. Berry couldn't hear what Jesus said, but he was blessed with an overwhelming amount of joy that he couldn't explain.

When they were through praying they all looked at Mr. Berry he was grinning so wide his cheeks ached. Light was shining from his eyes he felt like he would burst with joy.

"I feel so light, like I could float all the way to the ceiling just like a feather drifting upward. I feel as though a thousand pounds has been lifted off my shoulders. And I've noticed something else. My neck and back don't' hurt." Mr. Berry said surprised but grateful.

"That's God's healing touch Mr. Berry. A lot of times when people get saved they are also instantly healed. Jesus is smiling on you." Sarah said as she smiled and looked at Beth.

They all hugged and as they did Mr. Berry said, "Sarah I have another proposition for you." He knew she would not refuse this offer. "It just came to me."

"What's that; Mr. Berry?" Sarah asked, her blue eyes bursting with love as she smiled.

"I want to record you signing the angel song." Mr. Berry said. "But all the proceeds of the record will go to the ministry of your choice. I believe this song will touch a lot of hearts just like it has touched mine. And what better way to reach people than by radio and television. You might even be on the Ed Sullivan Show. I must be changed. The old Berry would never make an offer like this." He said and then laughed out loud. "I also want to add that if any sponsors pick you up and want to use you to promote their products that those proceeds will be put in a special trust fund for your college education." Mr. Berry was adamant about that.

Sarah still smiling said, "You are clever aren't you? I think that would be a super idea, I accept."

Mr. Berry was bursting with thankfulness and gratitude and said, "Now I'm God's child too and I believe He can use my talents as well. I'm so happy for what He's done for me today; I want to do something for Him." A true sign he was a brand new follower of Jesus.

They shook hands. Then Mr. Berry said. "That's great I'll have the necessary papers written up. In the meantime how can I learn more about this new Jesus I've just met? I know He isn't new, but He is new to me." Mr. Berry laughed with a joyful expression of love, earnestly wanting to know more.

Sarah picked up her bible. "You start with one of these Mr. Berry. Read Matthew, Mark, Luke and John. They walked with Jesus while he was on the earth and they can tell you first hand everything he did. Then find a good spirit filled church you'll want to be around family. And you can call Granny, Beth, Uncle George or me anytime. And one more thing you'll want to be baptized in water and in the Holy Spirit. You can read about that in the book of Acts. But not too much too fast everything will come in due time."

With tears in his eyes Mr. Berry said, "Thank you Sarah I appreciate that."

George reached out and gave Mr. Berry a great big hug patting him on the back he said, "Not only are we happy right now Mr. Berry, but there's a party going on in heaven. The Holy Angels are shouting and singing, *A New Babe in Christ has been born.*"

Hugging George in return, Mr. Berry said, "Really George? That thrills me knowing even the angels care when a soul is new born." Sarah and Beth got in on the hug too!

Sarah's Story

In the morning it flourisheth, and growth up; in the evening it is cut down, and withereth. Psalm 90 6

News about Sarah and Beth spread throughout the studio. Everyone wanted to hear the little girl angel sing, *The Angel Song*. The newspapers got wind of the story, Sarah was front page news. The headline said, **'Angel Girl Sings Angel Song.'**

Hearing the news, Sarah got down by her bed and prayed. *"Lord, you know I didn't want to be in the spotlight but Lord if this is your way of spreading your word, I'm your girl. I won't let you down. I love you Lord."*

It wasn't ten minutes after she prayed that a knock came at the front door. As George opened the door, two men stood there with camera and note pads.

"What can I do for you gentlemen?" George said curiously holding onto the door.

"Are you Mr. George Willis?" One of the men asked.

"Yes, and you are?" George asked.

"We would like to do an exclusive interview with Miss Sarah if that is alright with you. I am Tom Brown and this is Pete Morris. We are with *Young Talent's Magazine* and would like to meet Miss Sarah and Miss Beth. We received a call from Mr. Berry he said he thinks it would be a good idea to do a bio of the young singer and her best friend."

"Sure, you boys wait right here and I'll give you an answer in about five minutes." George left the room to let Sarah know two men from *Young Talent's Magazine* were here to see her and Beth.

"Thank you Mr. Willis." Tommy said. The two men walked over to the sofa and sat down.

George went to Sarah's door and knocked softly. He didn't want to disturb her if she was sleeping.

"Come in Uncle George. Beth is in the bathtub and I was praying. Who was at the door?" Sarah said as she composed herself.

"There are a couple of magazine guys that want to do an interview with you and Beth. Mr. Berry thought it would be a good idea. But if you don't want to, it'll be OK, I can have them leave. I really think it would be good for you though." George said with a determined expression.

"What? Oh yes. OK, but what do I say? What if I say the wrong thing?" Sarah was surprised, nervous and a little intimidated.

"Speak from your heart Sarah. You're good at that." Uncle George said then turned to leave.

"OK, if you think it's alright. I'll let Beth know what's going on too, tell them we'll be right out." Sarah ran a brush through her hair, smoothed her skirt and then tried to calmly walk to the living room. Both men stood to greet her as she entered the room.

"Hello Miss Sarah I'm Tom Brown and this is Pete Morris, we're from *Young Talent's Magazine*. It's nice to meet you. If you don't mind we'd like to do a story about you and Miss Beth. We've heard you've got quite a following. Would that be alright with you?" asked Tom.

"Well yes, that would be fine. It's nice to meet you too," Sarah said. She felt a little awkward but told herself to relax. She smiled and waited for their questions.

"Mr. Berry said he'd like for us to do an exclusive interview with you and Miss Beth. Do you know what that means?" Pete asked trying not to be too forceful. He knew she was nervous.

Sarah thought for a moment then said, "I think it means you guys are the only ones who get the inside scoop of our story. Is that right?"

I sure wish Beth would hurry up and get in here. I hope I don't say the wrong thing, she thought looking at the clock on the wall.

"You are exactly right. Will that be OK with you?" Pete asked as Tom looked at her trying to set her at ease. He put his pad and pencil down hoping she would not feel rushed.

Sarah looked at Uncle George. George nodded, yes.

Sarah sat tall and straight her blue eyes glowing. A yellow headband held her hair back. It matched her pale yellow blouse and brown pleated skirt. She became serious but inquisitive.

91

Breathing slower Sarah took a breath and asked, "OK, what do you want to know?"

Looking at Sarah with his bright eyes, Tom said, "This will be painless I promise. In your own words tell us where you came from, where you see yourself in ten years and what are some of your favorite activities?"

Sarah cleared her throat and thought, "This doesn't seem so bad," and said. *"I was born in a little town called Cedar Bluff, Alabama, I live there with my Granny. My mother died giving birth to me. And my dad died the day after I was born. I never got to meet either one. I guess you can see I'm different. My Granny calls me special because I have a White family and a Colored family. Sometimes kids make fun of me and call me mulatto but I don't mind I know they are just ignorant. My best friend is Beth she will be out in just a minute.*

The thing I love to do more than anything in the world is to play music and sing and tell others about my faith in Jesus, and how he loves them very much.

I'm like most other girls I like to go to the movies and listen to rock-n-roll music. I especially like Elvis Presley's new song Heartbreak Hotel. I also love to swim and fish.

In ten years…that's a long ways off. I do think about the future sometimes though. I see myself singing and traveling all around the world. Places like Africa, Ireland and to Israel. To walk where Jesus walked, that would be the most fascinating of all. Can I ask you both something?"

92

"Sure." The men answered in unison.

"Mr. Tom you go first. If you could go anywhere in the world and money was no object where would you go?" Sarah asked.

"That's a very good question. Let's see. I have always wanted to visit Paris. I suppose that's the romantic in me." Tom said with a snicker. "I'd like to see the Eiffel tower, but my biggest dream is to visit the shrine of Lourdes it's in south western France, where Our Lady of Lourdes appeared to Bernadette Soubious in 1858." Tommy had a faraway look on his face as he spoke.

"That would be lovely." Sarah said. "I've heard about the miracles that have happened there. I believe in miracles." Sarah was glad she had asked him, she liked his answer.

"What about you Mr. Pete where would you go?" Sarah asked.

"Hum? There are several places I've always wanted to go. One is to Egypt to see the pyramids and the other is to Alaska. They say that in Alaska, the longest day in the summertime last about nineteen hours. I also love to fish! I could do a whole lot of fishing in nineteen hours. Why do you ask?"

Sarah's eyes were bright as she looked at each man then said. *"I'm interested in people; I like to know who I'm talking to. Both of you lit up like a porch light, when you spoke from your heart about where you'd like to go."*

"You know something Sarah; you are very wise for one so young. How'd you get so smart?" Pete said as he put down his pen and really looked at her. "You'd make a great reporter." Pete said giving a little laugh.

"Mr. Pete, I guess it comes from reading the bible especially Psalms and Proverbs. My Granny is very wise too. She's the best Granny anyone could ask for." Sarah said with gratefulness in her heart.

"Sarah, tell us about your friend Beth." Pete said.

"Beth and I are more like sisters than friends. We were pretty much raised together born on the same day at the exact same time. Only she lives about four houses away from me. But in the summertime we're inseparable. She has a beautiful voice and also reads music and she plays the violin. We've been doing that since we were two years old. She's smart and bold and you sure don't want to make her mad. It's true what they say about red heads, sweet as apple pie but sour as a lemon if you cross em." Sarah laughed.

Pete and Tom laughed too and made notes on their note pads.

About that time Beth came into the room.

"You talk'n about me Sarah?" Eyes flashing...

"See what I mean?" Sarah said and she jumped up to give Beth a hug.

"Naw, I ain't talking about you very much..." Sarah said giving a wink.

Both men laughed again as they stood to greet Beth.

Pete spoke first. *"Beth we'd like to know where you see yourself in ten years."*

Beth sat down beside Sarah and said, *"Well my plan is to attend college and then onto the mission field probably to Africa. I've always had a heart for helping people. If that's God's will for me that's what I want to do.* Beth said with confidence.

"WOW, you girls sure know what you want." Tom said as he wrote in his notebook.

"We've been taught from an early age that the most important thing in the world is to know Jesus in a personal way. Then everything else will fall into place. The bible says the steps of a righteous man are ordered of the Lord. I guess that goes for girls too." Beth said smiling as she gracefully pushed her hair over her right shoulder. Her red hair against the bright blue blouse she wore accented her striking features that she was completely unaware of, freckles and all.

Tom snapped a picture as Beth talked and then he took one of Sarah.

"We don't want to keep you much longer but would you mind singing us a song?" Pete asked.

"Come on Beth lets sing Que Sera, Sera (Whatever will be, will be) and with that Sarah walked over to the piano.

"That's a good one we love Doris Day," They both said in agreement.

As the song came to an end, Tom and Pete clapped their hands enthusiastically. Tom looked at his watch then said, "Just one more favor and we'll be on our way."

Tom asked, "Sarah, in your own words tell us what you'd like the readers of this article to know about you."

Sarah with a serious expression bowed her head for a moment. "Well Mr. Tom I'd love for the readers to know that we are not a color, or mixed breeds. We are all from the same human race. When we are cut our blood runs red, we have feelings like anyone else. Ignorance causes fear and fear causes pain and the pain separates us from each other. There is a bridge that ties us all together, Jesus is that bridge. In Him we can agree and we can love each other without prejudice and hate.

I believe God put me here to help others to understand and know that bridge. The music carries us to the bridge and into the very presence of God. Only in knowing Jesus can we be set free from fear and prejudice.

The Angel song that my Uncle George wrote opens our hearts so that we can hear and understand God's grace and anointing. That anointing breaks down all the barriers of fear and pain and sends healing to our hearts. Shall I sing it for you now?" Sarah asked.

"Yes please do, we would love to hear the Angel song." Both men listened intently as Sarah sang.

The sound resonated throughout the whole room. It was as if the windows of heaven opened up and one humble angel was being heard. It pierced each man's heart and they knew they were in the presence of someone, other than an earthly being. It was, as if, God Himself had stood up. The love they felt, the peace unexplainable, they had never, ever experienced anything like this before, nor would they ever again. An undeniable transformation had taken place, they were touched, and they were set free, as they heard the angel sing. Only this was not an angel it was Sarah a little ten year old girl!

Tom and Pete were speechless. They were awe-struck, frozen some place between heaven and earth.

Then Pete said, "Sarah, you have an extraordinary gift. No doubt about it. You're the next Mahalia Jackson. You got my vote, no matter what, keep singing and doing what you do! I'm not a religious person but I can say this, you stirred my heart big time and I think you're swell!"

"Mr. Pete, Jesus isn't religious either, he wants you to know him; walk with him; talk with him. He wants to be, not only your best friend but your brother and more than that your, Savior. One day real soon you're going to meet Him in a very real way. Don't wait too long." Sarah said then looked straight into Pete's eyes and saw tears running down his face.

"OK, Sarah, I think that time is now, what do I do to make Jesus my best friend and Savior?" Pete asked.

Sarah took Pete by the hand and said, "Come on Beth let's pray. Repeat after me Pete."

Then she looked at Tom. He smiled and said, "Sarah this song reminded me of something I had forgotten or rather pushed aside for some time but I will be in church on Sunday. Thank you I'll never forget you. I'll be seeing you in the newspapers, and listening to you on the radio. I know Ed Sullivan will want you on his show. But most of all, thank you for sharing your faith with us. The article we're doing will reflect everything that was felt here today I'm proud to be part of your human race!" He hesitated a moment, his heart was pounding. Tommy said, "I want what Pete just received too!"

Sarah, Beth and Pete held hands. "Tom, repeat after me." Sarah said.

They all prayed. Tears flowed, angels rejoiced and two new souls received salvation.

"Sarah, Beth, thank you for everything we will stay in touch. We came here for an interview but we're leaving with a new life." Tom said as they headed out the door.

"We'll never forget you." Pete said as he gave each girl a friendly hug.

A copy of *Young Talent's Magazine* came in the mail to Sarah and Beth the article said. *"Meet Sarah and Beth they complement each other and share a tremendous, music ability. We had the privilege of meeting and interviewing them. Hold onto your hats because they have more to offer than just their music which is amazing in itself. Sarah and Beth are the best of friends born on the exact same day and time. They never meet a stranger and their faith and talent will leave you begging for more. Sarah is a born again Christian and is not shy about telling you about her Jesus. In fact that's the purpose of her life. She not only sings like an angel she is an angel. The color of her skin does not stop this little lady from the* call on her life. She's not the ordinary she is extraordinary. Her hope is to travel the world bringing Christ to all she meets. Beth is as strong and articulate in her faith as well and hopes to one day travel to Africa as a missionary. They are amazing young ladies. When asked what Sarah would like to say to you in this article this is what she said. "Tell them it's not about color it's about being what God wants you to be. It's about loving people. It's about obeying God and following the call on your life. Stop hurting each other and start loving one another." You'll want to be watching these two stars. Their lights will be shinning for a very long time. In fact they have a new song that will be released real soon. It's called the Angel Song. I know that after my meeting with them my life was changed forever! Get the record you'll be so glad you did.

Article by: Pete Morris and Tom Brown.

The Revelation

For we are consumed by thine anger, and by thy wrath are we troubled. Psalm 90:7

Months passed and the girls were back in school. George moved in with his sister Norma Jean. They waited patiently for word from Mr. Berry. Then one Friday afternoon in September the phone rang.

"Hello," said Sarah.

"Oh, hello Mr. Berry, yes hold on I'll get Granny." Sarah set the receiver down.

"Granny, Uncle George, come quick, Mr. Berry is on the phone hurry!" Then Sarah ran to turn on the radio.

Granny took the phone.

"Hello, alright I'll listen to the radio then I'll call you back." Granny hung up the phone and hurried to the living room.

Sarah and Uncle George were listening intently as Granny entered the room.

Granny's hand went to her throat, mouth open she gasped as she heard her granddaughter's voice over the radio. George was mesmerized and Sarah was in awe!

Beth came running into the house screaming. "Sarah! Sarah! You're on the radio!"

As the song finished playing…they all stood up hugging each other, tears running down their faces thrilled at what they had heard.

"I can't believe it. It was; it was my Sarah on the radio." Granny began to shout and dance about. Remembering she needed to call Mr. Berry back she scurried to the kitchen but as she was about to pick up the phone, it rang.

Picking up the phone she listened as Mr. Berry began to give her the details. "Hello, Norma Jean, this is Mr. Berry. We've been getting phone calls all morning the phone's been ringing off the hook! With this kind of exposure Sarah will go up in the charts in no time. I'll keep you posted on the progress. We need to get together. I flew in to Alabama last night so how does tomorrow sound? About 8:00a.m.?"

"That will be fine Mr. Berry come to the house and I'll make breakfast it'll be easier that way." Granny said wondering why all the rush.

"Great, see you then." Mr. Berry hung up the phone.

As soon as Granny hung up, the phone, rang again. The Mayor of Cedar Bluff was calling.

"Hello Norma Jean, I just heard Sarah singing on the radio. It was beautiful I want to sponsor her to make sure she has everything she needs to be a success." The mayor was very excited. "I'll pay all the expenses. What do you say?" asked Mayor Johnson.

Granny stood very still not knowing what to say. I can't believe it; the Mayor wants to sponsor Sarah, she thought. It took a few minutes for everything to sink in. "We'll need to pray about it Mayor." Granny said. "Yes, I'll talk to Sarah and George and let you know. As far as I know we'll meet with you tomorrow afternoon around 3:00. If anything changes I'll give you a call." Granny hung up the phone and looked at Sarah, Beth, and George, then said. "I declare God sure does work fast. Mayor Johnson wants to meet with us in his office tomorrow afternoon. He wants you to pray with him, Sarah, he said it's urgent. And he said the phone has not stopped ringing. They want to have a revival at the church and asked if you'll sing the angel song. People are crying and praying and want to get saved. They want to have the service this Sunday. I told him I'd have to ask you. What do you say?" Granny was out of breath with excitement. "And he wants to sponsor you; he said he'd pay for everything."

"Oh course we'll meet with him Granny, the Lord is doing everything we've been praying about. And if He wants me to sing that's exactly what I'll do." Sarah said and was delighted that God was moving so fast. "I won't need a sponsor everything is going to charity. But we can explain that to the mayor tomorrow." Sarah said.

The next morning they met with Mr. Berry and made all the necessary arrangements for Sarah to appear on the Ed Sullivan show in two weeks.

Afterwards they went to the Mayor's office and found a line of people standing on the sidewalk. As Sarah got out of the car a roar of cheers went up for her. She was startled. Everyone began clapping for her and wanted her autograph. Uncle George protected her and escorted her, Beth, and Granny into the building.

The Mayor greeted them and led them to his office. "Norma Jean this is really big and a great opportunity for Sarah but I'm sure you understand that. Y'all please have a seat. I have something very important to discuss with you." The Mayor rushed around like the place was on fire.

"Betty, hold all my calls. I don't want to be disturbed." The Mayor said as he closed the door.

"What's this all about Mayor?" Granny questioned.

"Yeah why have you asked us here today Mayor?" George asked curiously reinforcing Granny's question.

The Mayor looked at Sarah and began to cry like a baby. "Sarah, I want you to forgive me I said some terrible things about your mother and your Granny. I was foolish and mean. But hearing your song today I was reminded of a time long ago when I was a boy how I fell in love with someone but my parent's didn't approve. She was a lovely girl. But she was different not of the same caliber or so my folks thought. They forbade me to see her. It broke my heart and made me a bitter person. Forgive me Sarah, can you ever find it in your heart to forgive me? And you to Norma Jean, can you forgive me?" The mayor blew his nose and looked up hoping he could be forgiven.

103

Sarah and Granny were shocked. They had no idea what was going on. "Why would the Mayor act like this," Sarah wondered.

Sarah being a little surprised and perplexed answered. "Well of course Mayor Johnson but there's nothing to forgive."

"It's just that this song touched my heart in such a way I can't explain." The Mayor said. "Your voice and the words penetrate the soul. I can't forget it." The Mayor seemed truly touched and humbled by the angel song. Composing himself he said, "And something else, Norma Jean, I want to set up a scholarship for Sarah to attend a college of music would that be alright with you?" Mayor Johnson sat, as if, on pins waiting for her answer, fidgeting with papers on his desk.

George taking the scene in thought to himself, "The Mayor's behavior is highly unusual. It almost seems as if he's hiding something, but what?"

"Ah, certainly Mayor I don't know what to say." Norma Jean replied.

"Just say yes." Mayor Johnson said as he blew his nose again.

"Yes by all means," said Norma Jean. "But there's one thing Mayor, Sarah won't be getting any of the proceeds from the record. It's all going to charity."

The mayor stared for a moment then said, "Well then we won't worry about that. I still want her to have the scholarship. Will that be alright?"

"Yes I think she would appreciate that very much." Granny said praising the Lord in her heart looking at Sarah. She had wondered and prayed about how she was going to be able to pay for Sarah's college education.

"That's all I needed to hear. Now don't you worry about anything I'll take care of it and I'll see you in Church on Sunday." With that the mayor stood up, shook their hands and escorted them to the door.

Mayor Johnson called his secretary into his office and said, "Betty I'm going out of town until Sunday, take these papers and have them made out to Sarah Evans I want everything to be in perfect order by the time I get back." He looked a little tired and withdrawn as he handed her the papers.

"Alright Mayor I'll see to it right away." Betty said looking a little perplexed. "I wonder where he's off too?" she thought but didn't ask any questions. "He hasn't been himself lately but I can't worry about that now I've got too much work to do." She took the papers and left his office wondering about how she was going to get everything done in such short notice.

Sarah rode back to the house in silence. Pondering all these things in her heart as they entered the house she turned to Granny and said, "Granny I need to be alone for a while if you don't mind."

Beth was with them the whole time, Sarah looked at her and said, "You understand don't you Beth?" Sarah reached out and hugged her best friend. Beth knew Sarah was struggling with her feelings but didn't push her she just said, "Sure Sarah, I'll be home if you want to talk later." Beth returned the hug then left for home.

Sarah went to her room closed the door and knelt down by her bed and prayed. *"Lord, I don't understand all of this. I don't want people looking at me like I've done anything special. I only wanted to bring glory to you. To sing so souls will be saved. Lord what do you want me to do?"* Sarah sat very still before the Lord and waited.

There was only silence!

She waited for one hour before the Lord; then two; then three; tears began to run down her face. As she opened her eyes a beam of light came through her bedroom window and lit upon her bible that was opened on her dresser. As Sarah watched a light breeze turned the pages. She walked over to the dresser and saw *Esther 4:14 lit up. "For if thou altogether holdest thy peace at this time, then shall there enlargement and deliverance arise to the Jews from another place; but thou and thy father's house shall be destroyed; and who knoweth whether thou art come to the kingdom for such a time as this?" (King James Version.)* Joy exploded inside Sarah's heart. Sarah grabbed her bible and ran to show Granny and Uncle George what God had shown her but as she turned to go she realized the window had not been open. She clapped her hands together with glee and said, "Thank you Jesus." "Then I must speak up. I must sing so people will hear." God had spoken to her.

"Uncle George, Granny, look what God just showed me." Sarah said giving her bible to her grandmother pointing to (Esther

4:14) and read, *for such a time as this!* "I was praying and a light came through my window and fell on my bible as a breeze turned the pages to this passage. But the window was not open. There was no way a breeze could have turned the pages. It's a miracle."

Sarah was beside herself, excited that God had spoken so clearly to her. She looked at Granny and said, "I was afraid I was hurting God by bringing attention to myself. I never want to hurt Him!" Sarah slumped to the floor before her grandmother. "I'm amazed that God would give me a sign like this, it's unbelievable. I just hope that I never disappoint him.

Granny put her needle point down, looked at Sarah and said, "You aren't hurting God, you're making Him very happy. Don't you see He's using your singing and Uncle George's song to bring people to Him? You've been obedient to Him, and He wants to bless you."

"Oh Granny," Sarah broke down and cried. "I've been so torn."

"Look at me Sarah, this is your calling. You are not alone. You've got me and Uncle George and Beth to help you. Most of all you've got the good Lord right here with you. He even spoke to you directly in his word using a beam of light to point it out to you. Don't you see? I know you're young but God has given you wisdom and a whole lot of insight. Now stop this crying and start praising Him. And besides that, your mom and dad are very pleased with you too. Why; they are looking down from heaven and cheering for you at this very moment." Granny looked at Sarah with love and compassion. Staring straight into Sarah's eyes she added, "You're anointed Sarah, never, ever doubt that."

"But Granny, you don't understand, he said if I keep singing he'll kill Taffy and make trouble for you and Uncle George and he'll cut my face so no one will want to look at a blue eyed Negro!" Sarah was growing hysterical.

"Who said such a thing?" Granny asked feeling as if she had just been struck, she stared at Sarah in horror.

"Remember Uncle George I told you I was attacked? Well it happened again only this time it was a man." Sarah said as she began to cry.

"Last week someone attacked me when I went to the girl's bathroom at school. Beth had a dental appointment and was not at school and I had an emergency so I went by myself. No one was around I thought it looked safe enough."

Philomel, Sarah's guardian angel said, "No, Sarah, don't go by yourself." But I didn't pay attention to my gut feeling, I had no choice, it was an emergency, I had to go.

"Someone held me from behind. I couldn't see who it was but he smelled like rotten apples. He said my mother got what she deserved, going with a Negro, and all I am is a Negro with a white girls eyes. He slurred his words and I could smell alcohol on his breath. Granny I've been so scared." Sarah sobbed.

"Now, now, we will get to the bottom of this. I'm going to talk to the Mayor about all of this. Don't you worry child, God is on our side He will protect you. Go wash your face and lie down for a while. I'll make supper then when everyone has calmed down I'll call the mayor." Granny walked to the kitchen wringing her hands as she went, praying, "Lord, help us!"

Sarah was finally relieved she told Granny about the attack but wondered how the Mayor could help. He seemed sincere in his conversion but there was something that didn't seem right. He reminded her of someone but couldn't place him. She seemed suspicious of everyone lately. Was she losing her mind? She lay down on her bed, exhausted and fell asleep.

"George it's just like the devil to show his ugly head when God starts to move on people's hearts and their lives begin to change. We need reinforcements. I'll call the prayer chain you call Mr. Berry. Then I'll call the Mayor." Granny said determined to find out who would say and do such a thing. *"If God is for us who can be against us?" "I can do all things through Christ Jesus who strengthens me!"* she quoted the scriptures to herself.

"Alright Norma Jean but first lets pray." Uncle George took Granny by the hand and said, *"For we wrestle not against flesh and blood, but against principalities, against powers, against the rulers of the darkness of this world, against spiritual wickedness in high places. Ephesians 6:12, now let's pray."*

"Lord Jesus you are our strength and our refuge a very present help in time of need. We need you Lord to intervene in this situation. Sarah has been faithful to you, she's your child. We bind every hindering spirit, every lying tongue and all that is trying to come against her, it's not her they are coming against they are

coming against you Lord. You said the battle is not ours it's yours. We take authority over this devil and command him to cease he cannot touch your anointed ones he has to flee in the name of Jesus. We command that he leave right now and all his cohorts we bind you and cast you out in the name of Jesus. We thank you Jesus for being our protection, our high tower, our mighty fortress and for bringing this man to his knees. Amen."

The demon of fear sneered and spit, then jumped from his perch. Then the spirit of confusion ran back and forth, and demon prejudice, screamed in horror. They all vanished from the house.

"Thank you George I really don't know what I'd do without you. I thank the good Lord every day for sending you to us." Granny said as she wiped tears from her eyes. *Garth-el, Norma Jeans guardian angel, placed his hand on her shoulder and said, "Peace be still."*

"You're a blessing to me too Norma Jean I'm going to investigate on my own as well. Don't you worry about anything God, is on our side. I'll call Mr. Berry then you can call the prayer group and the Mayor." George said as he reached for the phone.

Stephen-arrow, Uncle George's guardian angel, smiled and placed his bow over his shoulder and relaxed. Knowing God was in control.

While Sarah slept she had a nightmare. She was sitting by a lake. The moon was full and she could hear crickets chirping. A dark shadow flew across the lake towards her and began to choke her. She couldn't cry out, she couldn't move at all. She stared into the darkest eyes she had ever seen. A snarling grin crossed the evil, scared face and a heart wrenching laugh came from the being of darkness. All she could do was struggle at first, but then something told her to relax and don't panic. Her body went limp. Her mind slowly began to fade. She could feel herself traveling in a tunnel the light was blinding. Her heart was pounding, as if she were on a roller coaster only traveling upwards. She couldn't breathe. Yet there was this sensation of amazing peace and joy. She realized she was standing upright then someone handed her a sword. But it wasn't an ordinary sword. There were sharp words shooting from a two edged blade, they were razor sharp on both sides. "It is written, get thee behind me Satan for God alone will I serve." "The Lord rebukes you Satan!" "God is for me you cannot come against me." "In the name of Jesus Christ of Nazareth you have to flee! Run! GO!" *Philomel, meaning the nightingale, Sarah's guardian angel, invaded Sarah's dream to help her.* All of a sudden Sarah's eyes flew open. She gasped for air. The demon vanished!

Sarah shouted, "Thank you Jesus!"

Philomel, hearing Sarah, bowed down on one knee to give homage to the Lord.

Granny and George came running into Sarah's room. "Sarah, are you alright? What's wrong?" They both scurried around her bed.

Sarah started laughing out loud and managed to say, "Oh Granny, Uncle George I'm not afraid anymore. Jesus gave me the power to overcome. I know exactly what to do now!"

The next morning Sarah got dressed and Uncle George drove her to school. Sarah met Beth in the hall and they walked to class together.

Entering the classroom someone tapped Sarah on the shoulder. Sarah looked straight into his eyes. Mr. Satani glared at her with black, vacant eyes. There was no light in him. He had a cold, blank stare.

"Sarah, I need for you to stay after school today to go over your exam." He said in a slow monotone voice.

Sarah could smell the alcohol on his breath and felt sick to her stomach. "I'm sorry Mr. Satani I have to go straight home after school. Uncle George is picking me up."

Mr. Satani's grip became tighter on her arm for a moment. *Philomel's head lifted in a start, the angel ever ready to protect Sarah but seeing there was no real threat she relaxed and said, "Pray in the name of Jesus, Sarah!"*

Sarah flinched and said in her mind, "In the name of Jesus let me go." Mr. Satani flinched and released her arm. *Two demon spirits that were always at Mr. Satani's side, slid to the back of the room and pouted. Still chained to the man, they waited.*

"Well alright then, I'll call your grandmother later and set up a conference. Now take your seat young lady." Mr. Satani moaned disapprovingly.

He walked to the back of the room and pulled a small flask from his pocket and took a drink known to the class as a tonic he took for his rheumatism. The demon alcohol gave a sneer and clutched Satani's arm once again.

Mr. Satani was a man in his late forty's. He had no family and had lived in Cedar Bluff all his life. He was a dark soul. There were strange stories told about him which made him interesting to the kids. His body was thin and he looked as if he'd break if he fell down. Thin, graying hair, that look glued to his ghoulish head, was slick and shiny from the grease he used to keep it in place.

He lived on the edge of town in what used to be a hotel. Gargoyles sat on each side of the entry gate. A pentagram hung over the gateway and he kept roosters and geese in his yard to ward off intruders. Or so he says. That didn't matter because no one wanted much to do with him anyway.

The only reason he had his job was because of his loving Christian mama, but she had died about ten years earlier. Her prayers were the only thing that kept him from completely being devoured by the demons. But they wouldn't give up and they drove him to the dark side. He was also known to read palms and tell fortunes. But that was done in secret. His mother's prayers were still working but it was still his decision. And he chose to listen to the lies.

Sarah relaxed and gave him a nervous smile and said, "Alright Mr. Satani I'll tell Granny." Then she took her seat.

Mr. Satani wiped the perspiration from his head. In a high pitched whiney voice he said, "Class take out your math books and practice your multiplication tables." He sneered, went to his desk and dozed off into oblivion. The students were used to this behavior

113

and didn't pay any attention to him. The bell rang and school was out. Everyone rushed out the door to be free from the reins of their captivity. Running in every direction they headed for an afternoon of freedom. Some were on bicycles, some walking but all thrilled to be going anyplace other than school. Sarah and Beth waved to Uncle George glad to have a ride home and out of the reach of danger.

"Uncle George greeted them and said, "How would you girls like an ice cream cone, my treat?" They both agreed that would be super.

As they drove away Sarah said, "Uncle George something pretty strange happened in Mr. Satani's class today." As Sarah explained what took place Uncle George said, "Sarah, the police came to the house this morning. Norma Jean told them about your attack. They said two other girls have reported that they have been threatened as well. Do you think Mr. Satani could be the one that attacked you?"

"No Uncle George, when I went to the bathroom that day, Mr. Satani was having a conversation with another teacher. It could not have been him. Besides even though he's a strange man he couldn't hurt a fly. He drinks way too much and his grip is too weak. He looks scary but he's a marsh mellow. This may sound odd but I have a suspicion I know who it was." Sarah said with a faraway look in her eyes.

"Sarah, if you know anything, you must tell the police." George said with a firm and concerned voice.

"Uncle George I know you are worried but I am confident that everything is going to be alright. God spoke to my heart the other night and said this is not unto death but will be for His glory. I have peace about it, don't worry. Everything is going to be revealed very soon." Sarah said with determination in her voice. "Have a little faith."

Philomel smiled. Shaking her head with amusement she thought, "Sarah is such a delight." The guardian angel was pleased to watch over her.

George was a little stunned and thought, "How can such a young girl have so much faith and wisdom?" Then he said all I'm saying is please be careful and don't trust anyone. This is serious."

Three days later Beth came to get Sarah to go to their favorite place where they liked to sort things out. They'd go to the little cave down by the lake. Sarah and Beth were talking about what had been going on when a cloud drifted in front of the sun blocking it and causing a shadow to move over them. A chill ran down Sarah's back.

"Beth we need to go." Sarah got up in a hurry.

"What's wrong?" Beth asked.

"It's a dream I had the other night. Come on hurry!" Sarah stood up and looked around she saw a masked man crouching in the trees looking at them.

"Beth, run!" Sarah shouted as she took off in a rush. Beth was right behind her. They ran all the way home, up the porch steps and into the kitchen screaming. "Granny, Uncle George!"

Granny and Uncle George were so startled that they dropped their coffee cups, which landed on the floor and shattered. Thankfully they were empty.

"What? What is it?" They both asked in exasperation.

"A man, a man in a mask was at the lake, he was watching us. He was hiding in the trees." Both girls screeched at the same time, both out of breath fear gripping them as they clung to Granny's arm.

Granny reached for the phone to call the police. "Just stay calm." But she was shaking herself.

"Norma Jean he'll be gone before they get here. I'll go and see what I can find out," said Uncle George.

A knock came at the back door. They all jumped and the girls squealed.

"Land sakes what's wrong with everybody?" A voice was heard from outside.

Granny shoved them all away and thought, "Norma Jean, get hold of yourself." Then she went to see who was knocking.

"Mr. Smith it's you, what's going on?" Granny asked.

"Norma Jean I may have scared the girls. I saw them run away. I didn't mean to give them a fright. I was in the woods down by the lake collecting herbs for my garden. I wear this mask because of my allergies. I'm so sorry if I caused a fuss." Mr. Smith said as he sat down on the porch swing gasping for air. "They scared me pretty good too. I didn't know what was going on."

116

"Oh, for heaven sakes, it's alright Mr. Smith. Some strange things have been going on around here lately and everyone is up in airs about someone making threats to some of the girls." Granny said.

Mr. Smith is a ninety two year old man who owns a small store and sells herbs and vegetables to the community.

"I would never hurt anyone Miss Norma Jean." Mr. Smith said, looking pale from rushing about in the heat.

"Never you mind Mr. Smith, it's alright no harm is done. George will drive you home you shouldn't be out in this heat." Granny said as she handed him a glass of water.

Sarah and Beth snickered and said, "We're so sorry Mr. Smith I guess our imaginations got the best of us. But with that mask on we didn't know who you were. The girls shook Mr. Smith's hand and said, "We won't be going to the lake for a while."

"That's a good idea." Uncle George said. Then he took his car keys from a nail on the wall and helped Mr. Smith to the car.

Over the next few weeks things seemed to settle back to normal. The routine of going to school, coming home, doing homework and mundane chores gave Sarah a false sense of security. She forgot about the threats and settled into practicing her piano and singing again.

Sarah watched the mailman drive up to the mailbox and put mail in the box before driving to the next stop. She ran to the mailbox to collect the mail. It was a letter addressed to her. *'Miss Sarah Evans'* it was an invitation to attend a concert at the Town

Hall with Mayor Johnson and his staff, for this coming Saturday. It said she would be picked up by the Mayor's driver at 6:00 p.m.

Granny looked at the invitation and said, "Oh my stars we've got to get you something nice to wear and fix your hair. This is an exciting event."

"Oh Granny thank you, I can't wait. I'll get to ride in the mayor's fancy car and go to a real grown up concert. Can Beth go shopping with us?" Sarah asked.

"Yes, you go get Beth and I'll finish washing up the dishes," Granny said as she hurried Sarah out the back door.

"George do you think it'll be alright for her go with the Mayor? He seems too eager sometimes. I get the feeling he's hiding something." Granny said as she put the dishes away.

"Well Norma Jean if you have doubts of course you should say so, but I think it'll be alright. There will be lots of people around and he seems to have had a real conversion," George said. He wasn't one to judge.

"I'm sure it's nothing." Granny said as she wiped her hands on her apron.

On the day of the concert, Beth came over to do Sarah's hair. She stood back and stared then she said, "Sarah you look lovely." Then she stuck in one last hairpin.

Sarah's hair was twisted into a sheik French twist which gave her a very grown up look. Her dress was blue chiffon and she wore little white pumps. Her Accessories were a string of pearls and tear drop pearl post earrings which complimented her lovely light brown skin.

Granny stood in the doorway to Sarah's room and gasped then said. "Sarah, you are dazzling. That blue dress brings out the blue in your eyes. Now you be sure to say thank you and remember your manners," Granny said as she wiped a tear from her eyes.

"The mayor's car is here." Uncle George yelled from the front room.

Sarah grabbed her clutch bag and ran to the door. She hugged everyone then ran out to the car. The driver held the car door open for Sarah to get in then she was gone.

At her arrival the Mayor greeted Sarah, extended his arm and led her to her seat.

"You look lovely Sarah. I remember your mother; you have her piercing blue eyes." The mayor said as he bent and kissed her on the cheek.

"Thank you Mayor Johnson. Did you know my mother well?" Sarah blushed.

"Yes we used to walk to school together. I'd carry her books. But we won't discuss that right now." He offered her a piece of hard candy. "Apple drops, would you like one?" The Mayor asked.

As Sarah reached for one she remembered the awful rotten apple smell when she was attacked. She gasped and dropped it.

"Sarah what's wrong? Don't you like apple drops?" The mayor's speech became slurred.

Sarah said, "Yes how clumsy of me." Sarah's heart began to pound, her mind raced. "I knew it! He's the one!"

Just then the concert began, the music drowned out all thought as she was caught up in a rush of terror and fright. What could she do? She must not panic.

"Jesus, help me!" She prayed with all her heart.

She could hardly sit still but she'd have to wait for the concert to end before she made her move to escape.

At the finale there was a standing ovation. Sarah made a dash for the isle but the Mayors hand gripped her arm, she was stuck.

The demon fear and anger gripped the mayor's head and hissed. "She won't escape this time. You've got her now."

Philomel tried to draw her sword, "Sarah, you have to pray I can't help you until you do."

The demons laughed at Philomel and then sneered, "You can't help her now, and you're powerless." A loud cold laugh filled the air as the demons celebrated their victory.

"Don't be so sure." Philomel thought to herself. "Come on Sarah pray."

Sarah was in a panic she couldn't think. *Demon confusion was swirling around her head.*

"Not so fast Sarah, you're not getting away this time, I have some place I want to take you." The mayor whispered.

As they made their way to the Mayor's car, Sarah tried desperately to find a way to escape. She needed a plan but confusion and fear held her captive. The mayor tied her hands and sat her in the front seat. They drove to a wooded area; the road was bumpy and curved many times. The moon was full but clouds hid it from view. Sarah tried desperately to get free but even if she did there was no one who could help her. Her heart pounded wildly. She twisted her hands but they were bound tight.

Finally she heard a still small voice within her heart say, *"Relax do not panic, I am with you. Remember the Angel song."* *Philomel said.*

"Yes, the angel song." Sarah thought.

"Praise to the Mighty Lord King of Heaven, Yeshua." *Philomel gave praise . Someone must be praying. The message got through to her.*

The Mayor had dismissed his driver. He drove Sarah to a secluded place it was dark and sinister. Even if she screamed no one would hear her.

"Just like your father Sarah, scared and weak. All he talked about was His God, His Jesus, so I sent him to meet them. How dare he take my girl from me? I loved your mother we were going to be man and wife but she chose a Negro over me. If I couldn't have her, neither would he. I smashed his head in and threw him in a ditch. He got what he deserved." The Mayor's eyes grew dark and he slurred his speech. Sweat poured from his brow. *Demon murder and hate laughed out loud. "Yes, yes, kill her!"*

Sarah started crying.

"Stop that you despicable little half breed. I only pretended to be sorry so I could get you alone. You'll never see the light of day again. Sarah, sweet little Sarah, voice of the angels. Well soon you'll be singing with the angels." The Mayor was full of anger and bitterness.

He came to a cemetery, stopped the car and got out. He grabbed Sarah and threw her to the ground. "Get up!" The mayor yelled. "I hate you! You should have never been born!" The mayor was angry and had gone mad. Sarah smelled the night air it was thick with fog. She smelled the rotten apple smell and gagged. Then a gentle breeze blew in her face clearing her thoughts. Granny and Uncle George were praying for her. Peacefulness came over Sarah and she began to sing the Angel song.

"Though times are hard…I'm by your side…Your tears I hold within my hand…"

"Stop that singing, you little brat." The mayor slapped her. "I said shut up you mulatto!" The mayor was in hysteria. Sarah winced at the pain but continued to sing. *No matter what I'll hold you close…Look to the one who understands…" Philomel's sword was drawn; she thrusts it into the mayor's heart.* The Mayor felt a sharp pain in his left arm he screamed in pain and grabbed his chest. He fell to one knee then the other.

"Oh God, help me!" He said through gritted teeth.

The demons screamed in terror. "NO!" But to no avail. The saints of God were praying. God send your warring angels to help Sarah, spare her life Lord and deliver her from evil.
Sarah continued to sing. *"Though fears may come and tears may fall…Be still and know that I am God…let perfect peace restore your*

heart...and know my love we'll never part..." The mayor was tormented torn by guilt and hate...the angels and the demons kept battling and Sarah kept singing.

"I walked the road of trials and torment...I sat with those who love me still...But on the cross...I felt the suffering...Of all the ones who loved me most..."

"God help me, save me, I don't want to die...not like this...I was wrong...I loved Jenny but she loved someone else...I couldn't let him live...I'm sorry...please forgive me...Sarah forgive me..." The Mayor was in agony and cried out in despair, "I can see David's face the shock the pleading in his eyes I killed him...I killed him..."

Philomel and thirty more angels were fighting the demons as they cried out in ugly, disgusting screeches. "He belongs to us, you can't have him, and you can't save this one. We will not give him up!" But they were disintegrating fast. Sarah kept on singing. Prayers increased the battle was raging.

"The birds they sing a nightly chorus of joy and peace to all they bring...so lift your voice and head toward heaven...and learn their song, their song and sing...He gives me peace, He gives me life, the angels sing be glorified, Praise to the King, our mighty King, We're going home on angels wings.

It was midnight the mayor fell on his back he couldn't move the pain was too great! "God I'll do whatever you ask...God I'm sorry..." Sweat poured from his body he was going to die and he knew what would happen after that. Darkness and lava would be his tomb. Torment for all eternity. He knew that much from the days he attended Sunday school. "It's too late! It's too late!" He cried out and wreathed in pain.

Philomel said, "Keep singing Sarah don't stop!"

"When in the stillness now at midnight, I see the stars of love so bright, I'll never ever doubt my Savior, For He will lead me through the night..." Sarah kept singing. The Mayor kept pleading.

He could hear the demons mocking him.... *"That's right Johnson, no one can help you now you're a murderer, and a hypocrite...you're mine now!"* And then Mayor Johnson screamed, "Jesus, save me!" The Mayor cried out in terror!

That was the final straw. Philomel saw her opportunity. She made a wild dash slashing the demons with her sword. They scattered screaming as they fled in terror.

"Victory shouted Philomel."

Norma Jean had called more prayer warriors. The battle was won. Sarah felt a release, and then finished the song.

"And on the breeze I hear him whisper, Press on my child and do not weep, for at the dawn you'll have your answer, so close your eyes and go to sleep..."

The Mayor lost consciousness. Police cars surrounded them lights flashing sirens blaring. They had a tip that the Mayor wanted to kill Sarah.

Sarah sat quietly in the dark starlit night as the attendants took her vital signs. She didn't say anything. She knew that Jesus had protected her, she was safe. She watched as the ambulance came and took Mayor Johnson away. She didn't know at the time if he had survived or not.

Sarah said a prayer for him, "Lord, I know what he did and I forgive him. I hope you will forgive him too!" Sarah lay back in the police car, exhausted, she fell asleep.

The next morning Sarah awoke in her own bed. Beth was sitting beside her and said. "Sarah, thank God you're awake. I was so afraid I'd lost you. We got news that you had been kidnapped. The Mayor left a note about what he intended to do, it was horrible. They said he was going to kill you then kill himself. He couldn't live with what he had done anymore. Granny and Uncle George began to call on everyone to pray. Then the Mayor's driver thought it was odd that he was sent home. He had left his house key in the Mayor's office so he went there to get his key and found the note. Thank goodness or they would have never found you. I'm sorry Sarah, are you alright?" Beth was out of breath and sobbing.

Sarah gaining composure said, "Beth it was amazing. At first I was terrified and I thought I was going to die. But a peace came over me and I was reminded to sing *the Angel song*. There was a battle going on between God, the devil and the Mayor. God used the song to destroy the hold on Mayor Johnson. Did he make it?" Sarah said as she sat up.

Philomel sat next to Sarah with love in her eyes for her dear sweet girl. "Someday we'll meet face to face, what a joy that day will be." Philomel thought.

Beth hugged Sarah and said, "Yes, he's arrested but he's in an Intensive Care Unit. The doctor said it's a miracle he's alive.

"You know what Beth, I was so scared at first but then I knew Jesus was with me and that he'd protect me and bring me through to safety. I may have brown skin and blue eyes. People may say that I sing like an angel. But one things for sure I will never ever doubt my Jesus; He will keep me through the night. Sarah sang the last verse of *the Angel Song*.

I wake at dawn and have my answer…His peace I sing to all who wait…And then He gives me sweet assurance…I'll never, ever be alone…These souls I bring to heaven's harvest…They are the ones who overcome…And now my love…You have your answer…

Your journey's only just begun!

The Testimony

Thou hast set our iniquities before thee, our secret sins in the light of thy countenance. Psalm 90:8

The mayor recovered from his heart attack and confessed to everything he had done. He was sentenced to life in prison. But that didn't matter because he was truly changed that night. He told the story to anyone that would listen to him.

Because of the drastic change in him the warden wanted to hear his testimony first hand. "What happened to you Johnson? What made the change?" The warden asked.

"Warden, I was going to kill Sarah Evans that was my plan and then I was going to kill myself. I couldn't live with the guilt and shame of what I had done so many years ago. I tried to justify my actions but there was no justification for what I did. On the night of Sarah's abduction she began to sing. It was as if ten thousand angels were singing. It was an overpowering thunderous sound. It came from within my body pounding and roaring and I could not make it stop. I thought my heart was going to explode. All I could think of, was if I died, I was going straight to hell. So I began to cry out to the only one who could save me. And then I saw Him. Jesus was as real as I am to you right now. He had the saddest eyes then they turned to anger, a piercing blinding light came from them. I was reduced to a groveling, disgusting worm. Wiggling and squirming in my own filth. I was dirty and putrid. Then I heard another voice. It was pure evil and vile. He was laughing and snarling and skipping about, "He kept saying you're mine you prejudiced degenerate, you murderer, there's nothing you can do to get away."

But the Angel song, the words, they penetrated the demons barrier, and I cried out for Jesus! Then all went black. I was falling down, down; down into an abyss of fire and darkness. Fire so hot it sent steam and lava rolling in every direction. The only light that shone was from the molten rock and I screamed, "Jesus, save me!"

Suddenly I felt a hand reach out and pull me upward.

"No!" The demon screeched in a horrifying hiss.

"Just before I woke up I heard Jesus say these words."

"I am the resurrection, and the life: he that believeth in me, though he was dead, yet shall he live: And whosoever liveth and believeth in me shall never die. Believest thou this?" (John 11:25-26)

I said, "Yes, Lord I believe!" Later I found his words in the book of St. John 11:25-26.

I woke up in the hospital and remembered everything that happened. "I will never forget it! I'll spend the rest of my life telling this story and thank God every day for a second chance. I can't change what I did to Sarah and her family. I'll have to live with that too, all I can do is hope for her forgiveness and tell people, Hell is real, but Jesus can save you from going there if you ask him too!"

The warden listened intently to the story. He was a man of fifty-nine years, round belly and balding head. The men knew he was not one to be toyed with or lied too. He could see right through lies. He had dealt with criminals for over thirty years. He knew something was different about Mayor Edward Johnson. After listening to the story he said.

"Mayor, *everyone continued to call him Mayor,* it's been two years now and I never tire of hearing your story. I can see how this has affected you and I can understand how it would. I've watched many of the men that have come here listen to your story too, and I see how it has caused many of them to change as well. I've been praying about something and I wonder if you would agree. I want to open a chapel here in the prison I'd like for you to be the director. It would be a way for you to share your testimony with those who are hurting and seeking as well. What do you say?"

"Warden I would like that," said the Mayor. "Most of the men in here poke fun; some have even threatened to kill me. But I don't care about that, I know what I have and I know Jesus. No one or nothing can take that from me." The mayor said with determination and conviction.

"I believe you Mayor or I'd never ask you to do this." The warden said then shook his hand. "We'll get started right away."

"Warden I wonder if you would do something for me." The Mayor said.

"What's that Mayor?" The warden asked.

"First of all please call me Ed I don't deserve the title of Mayor. Second, I want to write a letter to Miss Sarah and ask if she'll come sing the Angel song." Ed said with compassion in his voice.

"Ed, I think that would be an excellent idea. Write the letter I'll see that she gets it. Now you watch yourself it's not going to be an easy task but I know God is with you." The warden said as he stood signifying the meeting was over.

"Thank you warden I'll do that." Ed said then he was led back to his cell.

Sarah and Her Peers

For all our days are passed away in the wrath: we spend our years as a tale that is told. Psalm 90:9

Sarah took a deep breath and blew out the candles on her birthday cake. Then Beth blew hers out. Thirteen years they had been celebrating their birthdays together. The back yard looked like a party store. Red, blue, green, yellow and pink balloons were tied to trees. Streamers hung in half loops around tables with pink table clothes. A two tier cake with yellow roses was served with strawberry, vanilla and chocolate ice cream. The girls giggled and watched as the boys played *pin the tail on the donkey*; then everyone joined in playing red light, green light; and hide and seek.

Tommy began to count, "One, two….nineteen, twenty, ready or not here I come!" Everyone scattered hunting a place to hide. Sarah ran behind the house and slipped into the pump house. But as she did she heard Jimmy grunt.

"Ow, Sarah, that was my foot you stepped on. I found this place first, now scat!" Jimmy whispered in an annoyed voice.

"It's too late Jimmy move over, if he hears you he's gonna catch us." Sarah shoved Jimmy over so that she could fit in the tiny space as well. She didn't care at the moment that they were so close; she was too focused on not getting caught by Tommy.

"Sh, I hear him coming." Jimmy whispered once more.

They stood frozen, so close they were breathing on each other. They waited with anticipation for Tommy's approach.

Tommy ran past the pump house and yelled, "I see you Susie Cooper. He chased Susie down and caught her before she could get to base. "Tag, you're it."

Sarah and Jimmy both let out a sigh of relief.

Tommy dashed out again to find Betsy, then Beth, saving Jimmy and Sarah for last. He rounded a tree and saw Betsy's foot…slowly reaching around the old oak he tagged her. "Tag you're it!"

Betsy screamed and tried to run, too late. "Tommmmyyy, no fair you cheated!"

"I did not Betsy Clark. I got you fair and square." Tommy yelled back at her.

Beth was hiding in the dog house, Taffy gave her away. "Taffy go on, you're going to get me caught."

"No use Beth I got'cha, come on out!" Tommy said feeling proud of himself.

"Oh alright, Tommy, you win." Beth was not one to give up but she was tired of playing the silly game anyway. She climbed out of the dog house and walked back to home base.

Tommy ran calling out, "I'm coming to get you Jimmy and Lotto." Tommy was hot and sweaty as he ran around the yard.

"I'm saving the best for last!" He thought as he surveyed every nook and cranny. "The pump house…ready or not here I come." A smirk crossed his face.

Jimmy was getting uncomfortable being that close to Sarah. "She smells just like honey suckles. Stop it get hold of yourself." He thought. His hands began to sweat. Sarah stood with her back to him. She turned slightly and as she did her cheek grazed his mouth. They both gasped and held their breath for a brief moment. Jimmy had to think of something fast. "Sarah, you run to the right and I'll run to the left he can't get us both." Jimmy said real quiet like.

"Alright Jimmy, on three; one, two, three!" They flew out of the pump house like birds being flushed from a thicket.

Only Sarah ran smack dab into Tommy. As he fell to the ground she let out a shrill scream. Leaving Tommy completely dumbfounded. Sarah, stunned for a moment caught her breath then took off running to home base. Jimmy was there waiting. They both laughed; happy they had out smarted Tommy.

After the games they sat around a bon fire and sang songs. They watched as fireflies flickered in the dim light like tiny fairies' on a quest and with awe they watched a shooting star race into the night leaving only a trace of star dust behind.

"Quick, make a wish!" Jimmy said to Sarah. Tommy rolled his eyes. "Jimmy you gett'n sweet on Lotto or something?"

"Oh mind your own business Tommy. You're just jealous." Jimmy said.

"No I'm not, you take that back or I'll knock your teeth out," Tommy yelled. He got mad and sulked.

"Don't be a drag Tommy." Jimmy said.

"Aw alright just forget about it. I'm cool." Tommy said.

It was late when Uncle George called for everyone to come to the house.

"Kids thanks for coming out today we've enjoyed having you. We'll see you in church tomorrow." George gave them all a hand shake as he led them out the door.

Sarah and Beth hugged each one and thanked everyone for coming.

"See ya tomorrow," the girls said as they watched everyone leave.

Jimmy was the last to leave. "Sarah." He said with his head bowed. "Yes, Jimmy, what is it?" Sarah smiled. Jimmy was shy, "Uh, Uh, see ya tomorrow Lotto!" And he scooted out the door.

On Monday morning Sarah sat on the porch and watched as the mailman dropped off the mail. Granny sorted the letters and said, "Hum this is interesting, here's one for you Sarah."

Sarah opened the letter. She grew a little pale. "What is it Sarah?" Granny asked with concern. Sarah was stunned and handed Granny the letter without saying a word.

Dear Miss Sarah,

I know I'm the last person you'd want to hear from, but I have an urgent request to ask of you. If it's alright with your grandmother and your Uncle George I'd like to ask if you'd come sing the angel song here in the prison. Let me explain. It's been two years and I still can't get over what happened to me. I tell everyone in here about Jesus and how he used your song to deliver me. I know I'll never get out of this place and that's alright. I'm right where God wants me and I wouldn't have it any other way. I hope you can find it in your heart to forgive me for what I did to you Miss Sarah. I don't even have the right to ask you. But God has put this on my heart and has assured me that it's his will. But it's still up to you if you accept or not. The warden is a Christian man and thinks it would be wonderful if you'd come. There are so many lost people here. Will you pray about it and let me know. Thank you Miss Sarah, please pray real hard.

Forever in your debt,

Ed Johnson

Granny looked up from reading the letter and said, "Well that's something to pray about for sure?" She said with a sigh, and then handed the letter back to Sarah.

Sarah took the letter and went to her room and began to pray. "*Lord Jesus, I know you said to forgive or we won't be forgiven. I know you have used the angel song many times and Lord I believe you. If this is what you want me to do I am more than willing but would you give me a confirmation. I want what you want Lord. Amen.*"

It wasn't one minute after Sarah prayed that the phone rang. "Sarah it's for you." Granny called from the living room. Sarah went to get the phone.

"Hello. Yes this is Sarah Evans. Oh hello Mr. Berry. What? You want to take me to the prison to sing the Angel Song! How did you…? God spoke to you, and told you to call me? Yes, I understand I was praying and asked God for a confirmation about that, just now! OK, as soon as I hang up the phone I'll write Mr. Johnson and get all the information and let you know. Thank you, Mr. Berry, I'll be sure to let Granny know. Good Bye!" Sarah hung up the phone and explained it all to Granny.

"Well if that's what the Lord wants, it's certainly alright with me. Of course Beth and your Uncle George will go too." Granny looked up toward heaven and said, "Thank you Jesus."

"Of course they will." Sarah ran to tell Beth the news.

Prison Doors Wide Open

The days of our years are threescore years and ten; and if by reason of strength they be fourscore years, yet is their strength labour and sorrow; for it is soon cut off, and we fly away.
Psalm 90:10

Three weeks later, Mr. Berry went to get Sarah, Beth and Uncle George to go to the prison. The warden welcomed them and escorted them to the hall where Sarah would sing. Sarah's heart beat a little faster and she felt as if butterflies where fluttering around and around in her tummy. Sarah took Beth by the hand and led her to a corner of the room. Beth knew exactly what Sarah needed. Beth bowed her head, placed her hand on Sarah's shoulder and began to pray.

"Lord Jesus, we know it's your will for us to be here today. We bind any hindering spirits that would try to disrupt what you want to do and we ask that the Holy Spirit manifest in the way that only He knows how. Be with Sarah as she sings and bring honor and glory to your name. Open these men's hearts and let them receive

your salvation. Amen." Beth gave Sarah a hug and said, *"You can do this."*

An angel named Zee-el, bold and sassy, with bright red hair that was pulled back in one long braid, hung behind her back; she grinned and pulled her cross bow ready for battle. There were other angels, as well, that stood around the room ready and waiting.

The room began to fill up. There were about 300 men sitting and staring at this little mulatto girl. Some looked very thin and hardened by life. Some were short and had no teeth. But this one man looked like the devil himself. His hair was long and stringy and tattoos of skulls and cross bones covered both arms. He had beady eyes, black as night. A large scar etched over one cheek bone and an eerie grin was plastered on his face. Sarah swallowed hard, her mouth went dry but she didn't reveal it to anyone around her. "Lord, give me your grace." She prayed.

The demon intimidation crouched on the man's shoulder. He hissed and dug his talons deeper into the man's neck. His eyes became like two molten rocks, with pointed teeth sharp as a razor; he sneered and spit came from his mouth then he said, "Look at me Sarah the demon hissed. You can't sing here today. These men will eat you alive. You're finished; you'll never get through your song! You're just a m u l a t t o...they don't want your kind here." These were the thoughts Sarah had as she looked deep into the man's eyes.

Demon intimidation would not budge. Zee-el shot an arrow at the foot of the man hitting his mark. The man grabbed his foot and winced in pain. *Intimidation stuttered "wha...wha...ttt"...and spit but was silenced.*

Sarah stepped to the piano but before she sat down she said, "Good afternoon gentlemen. I want you all to stand up and hold hands." She had the confidence of David the shepherd boy who stood before Goliath with just a few stones and a sling. She didn't back down. She knew in whom she believed and who was fighting this battle. The God of Abraham, Isaak and Jacob, she had the Holy Ghost on the inside of her. She was not afraid!

The men looked first at Sarah in disbelief then at each other and scoffed and grunted. "No way, I'm not doing that." They all agreed. These were not gentlemen. They were criminals, thieves, liars, murders, drug lords. They were tough and no little mulatto girl was going to make them hold hands.

"Not with these scum-bags." One man cried out.

Sarah thought, if Jesus could save a thief on the cross surely he could save these men too.

Sarah raised her hands and eyes toward heaven and shouted. "In the name of Jesus Christ of Nazareth be gone, you fowl demons. You have no place here. Leave!" The men stood up, grabbed each other's hands, bowed their heads and waited. It was like lightning striking their souls.

Demons screamed, scattered and fled at the mention of Jesus's name. Angels of love, peace and protection pulled their swords and swung until the room was cleared. Peacefulness settled over everyone.

Sarah said, "You may be seated." She said, "Thank you Jesus." She knew who her help came from. She then took her seat at her designated spot.

She sat down at the piano and from the very first note everyone in the room became silent. As she sang the angel song tears began to run down faces. Great sobs began to resonate around the room. The Holy Spirit began to move on hearts, the devil looking man was the first to go to the altar. "Oh God forgive me. I've been a wicked man. I need you. I'm sorry. Great sobs shook his chest. I never knew anyone could love me. I never thought anyone cared." Ed Johnson went to him and wrapped his arms around the man and prayed with him. He accepted Jesus as his personal Lord and Savior. A total of two hundred and fifty men came forward crying and asked to be saved. The others had questions but didn't make the decision that day but they were deeply touched. Hearts were softened, lives were changed.

An inmate stood up and said, "Miss Sarah I may not be pardoned from my life sentence for what I did, but I know Jesus pardoned me today and for all eternity. Thank you for coming and singing today."

Another man stood also and said, "Yeah and thank for the bible. I've never had a bible of my very own. I'm gona keep it with me always."

Sarah smiled and said, "Thank you for responding to the Lord. I hope you'll always remember it's Him who gets all the glory.

Read your bible and pray. He'll keep you on the straight and narrow path."

Men all around the room nodded their heads in agreement and said, "You bet we will."

Sarah also gave them an autographed copy of the Angel Song along with a Certificate of Salvation. The men gave her a standing ovation and thanked her for coming.

After the service, Sarah went to see Mr. Johnson. She shook his hand and said, "Mr. Johnson you are no longer the person that you once were. I can see that. I do forgive you but most of all God has forgiven you. Thank you for allowing me to be a part of this service today. God has called you to a battle field of the greatest need. I will be praying for you."

"Thank you Miss Sarah, that means a lot to me. God did a mighty work here today and as you know the Angel song is mightily anointed." Mr. Johnson said with tears in his eyes as he shook Sarah's hand. "I can see great things in your future. I pray God's protection and long life for you Miss Sarah. I'll never forget how God saved me when all I deserved was death. Oh and one more thing, Go to the Mayor's office I was serious about getting you a full scholarship. It's there waiting for you."

"What, really, thank you so much I don't know what to say?" Sarah said stunned. "Do something for me Mr. Johnson, be sure and pray in the Holy Ghost, he knows what's needed more than we do. Don't get discouraged. Jesus is on your side now. His holy angels are protecting and guiding you. With the help of Jesus we won a battle today, but more are coming." Sarah kissed him on the cheek and said, "Thanks again."

Bowing his head Mr. Johnson humbly received her kiss with gratitude and amazement. "God bless you Miss Sarah. I'll never forget you."

Light Passes

Who knoweth the power of thine anger? Even according to thy fear, so is thy wrath. Psalm 90:11

Sarah stood looking into the casket and thought back to four years ago remembering how God had turned someone so vile, into a His child and how this man had touched so many lives. She smiled thinking fondly of Mr. Ed Johnson knowing he was now with the angels. His favorite scripture verse was; *He that dwelleth in the secret place of the most High shall abide under the shadow of the Almighty. Psalm 91:1*

Philomel turned to Sarah and said, "Yes Sarah, he sure is. He's rejoicing down by the river even now."

Sarah felt an assurance and peace settle over her spirit. A song of praise rose up on the inside of her as she sang. *Peace, peace, wonderful peace coming down from the father above, sweep over my spirit forever I pray...then hummed the rest of the tune silently.*

The warden standing beside Sarah said, "That was lovely Sarah. Ed was a devout servant of the Lord, it wasn't right what happened to him but there was nothing we could do he was dead before we could get to him. Someone poisoned him. The ring leader thought by killing Ed he'd shut the "Christians" up, but this has made them even stronger. We had to separate the two groups. There are some people whose hearts are too hardened and will never change. Ed did a lot of good within these prison walls. He will be greatly missed."

"I'm so very sorry Warden; God has his reasons for allowing things to happen. All I know is that where Mr. Johnson is now, he'd never want to come back here after spending one moment in the presence of the Lord. We can't bring him back but one day we'll see him again."

"Is there anything that needs to be done? Do you need anything?" Sarah asked.

"No, Miss Sarah just continue to pray, you've been a life safer coming here and singing the Angel Song. Ed loved that song and he loved you too Miss Sarah. Don't you worry about anything God's will, will be done. You keep in touch; let me know how you're doing. You've got a long journey ahead of you. I'll be praying for you too." The warden said with encouragement and appreciation in his voice.

"Thank you warden I appreciate that. As a matter of fact I'll be singing in Birmingham next week, there's a big church there that needs some shaking up." Sarah smiled and gave the warden a wink.

"Be safe on your trip back home." The warden and Sarah hugged. "I will sir, God bless you."

Sarah and Uncle George arrived back home at midnight. Granny was waiting up. I made you some tea and hot coffee.

"It's been a long day Norma Jean I'm going to hit the sack." Uncle George said as he gave her a hug and headed for his room.

"Good night, George." Granny said. "I'll see you in the morning."

Sarah hugged Granny. Taking a cup of tea she sat down and said, "Granny why does life have to be so complicated?"

"What do you mean Sarah?" Granny said as she yawned.

"Well if mama hadn't been with my daddy then Mr. Johnson wouldn't have killed him and I wouldn't have been born and none of this would have happened. Now, mama, daddy and Mr. Johnson are gone. What's going to become of me?" Sarah said as she sat on the couch. Covering her face with her hands she cried. She stopped for a moment and said, "Mr. Johnson said he got me a full scholarship. I was stunned. I guess I have that to count on. After everything that has happened I just have a hard time believing sometimes how God works in our lives." Sarah wiped her eyes and looked a little bewildered.

"Well praise the Lord for that." Granny said. "That's certainly something to be thankful for. At least you have that. Now dry those tears." Looking at Sarah she said, "Honey you're tired it's been a long day. Let's get a good night sleep and if you're still feeling discouraged tomorrow we'll have a nice long talk OK?" Granny said as she put her arm around Sarah and helped her to her feet.

"Alright Granny, you're right I am tired." Sarah stopped crying, hugged her Granny, "I know you're tired too. I'm sorry for acting like a big baby." Sarah said, Right after I help you clean up this mess I'll go to bed."

"No, I'll just put everything in the sink and I'll do it in the morning. Sleep now." Granny said wearily, shewing her granddaughter to bed.

The next morning a knock came to Sarah's bedroom door. Sarah rolled over, still under the covers. "Come in." Sarah said sleepily.

Opening the door Beth asked, "Sarah, are you still sleeping?" Beth plopped down on the bed.

"Well I'm not now." Sarah said. Stretching her arms over her head and yawning. "What are you doing here so early?" Sarah asked.

"It's Saturday and guess what's playing at the theater?" Beth said with excitement.

"So early, it's 9:30 in the morning; remember its Saturday? We said we'd go to the theater to see that new scary movie that's out!" Beth said excited and a little irritated at her friend.

"Beth I'm tired. We didn't get home til midnight. Can't you come back later?" Sarah was whinny.

"Sarah! No way! The box office will be sold out. It's Psycho, With Janet Leigh and Anthony Perkins. Come on get up!" Beth was not going to take no for an answer. "Besides Jimmy and Tommy are meeting us there."

146

Sarah threw back the covers and shot out of bed like her pants were on fire. "Well why didn't you say so? Give me thirty minutes." Sarah ran to the bathroom to get ready.

Beth picked up a magazine and waited.

"Granny, Beth and I are going to the theater. There's a new movie we want to see." Sarah said as she slipped on her shoes.

"Oh, what are you going to see?" Granny said as she looked up from folding towels. "I thought she wanted to talk about life." Granny thought and giggled to herself.

"It's the one with Janet Leigh that everyone is talking about." Beth said.

"You don't mean Psycho?" Granny said with a disapproving look. "Sarah don't you think that will give you night mares?"

"Oh Granny, it's just a movie and besides Jimmy and Tommy are going to meet us there. It's just for fun." Sarah said hurrying out the door.

"I know you'll want to get a sundae afterwards but don't be gone all day." Granny shouted, staring in disbelief as they went out the back door. "Those two, I just don't know what's to become of them." Granny thought and laughed to herself.

"Ok Granny, see ya later," they yelled as they ran to get in the car where Mrs. M. was waiting.

Mrs. M. dropped them off in front of the theater and said, "I'll be back in a few hours to pick you up. I know you'll be getting ice cream with the boys afterwards. Tell Tommy and Jimmy I'll take them home too!"

"Thanks mom." Beth said.

"Yes thanks Mrs. M. you're super," Sarah said as she got out of the car.

"I hope you girls know what you're doing, seeing this movie. Don't come crying to me when you can't get in the shower, ever again," Mrs. M said. She saw the boys and watched as they all went inside then drove away.

The Temptation

So teach us to number our days, that we may apply our hearts to wisdom. Psalm 90:12

"Beth, Sarah!" Tommy waved, "Over here. We already got the tickets."

Normally Sarah would not have been able to sit with her friends there was a section in the balcony for coloreds, mulattos included. But Mr. Thompson, the owner made an exception for Sarah. She was a town celebrity although Sarah didn't realize why he thought that. She didn't see herself as a celebrity. She was only doing what God wanted her to do.

"You kids get ready to scream." Mr. Thompson said using his flashlight to point the girls to their seats.

"Mr. Thompson," said Sarah, "Jimmy and Tommy will be here in a few minutes can you let him know where we're seated."

"By all means your highness!" Mr. Thompson said sarcastically. He was a little irritated that he let Sarah sit with her friends. "If you aren't careful I'll make you sit upstairs with the others of your kind girly!"

Sarah just ignored his statement. She was used to him being rude. "Thank you sir, I appreciate your generosity."

He grunted, "I don't want any problems." Then he left in a huff.

Tommy and Jimmy went to the concession stand they ordered two large bags of popcorn, a box of twizzlers and four drinks.

Mr. Thompson was waiting with his flashlight. "Follow me boys, your highnesses are waiting."

Walking down the aisle they spotted the girls. "Now I don't want any problems out of you kids, mind your manners." They never gave him any trouble but it was just his way of badgering. "Keep your hands to yourselves or I'll see to it your parents know about it."

"Yes sir." They all agreed.

Tommy sat next to Beth and Jimmy sat next to Sarah. The lights went out and they sat in anticipation waiting and watching. As Janet Leigh got into the shower and was about to scream, Sarah and Beth threw their hands over their eyes. Tommy and Jimmy held onto the girls and they all screamed.

After the movie they walked out of the theater wide eyed and in shock. "That was horrible." Beth said.

"Yeah, your mom was right. I'll never be able to take a shower again." said Sarah.

Tommy and Jimmy tried to man up but they were both shook up pretty bad. "Come on Jimmy lets go get some ice cream." Tommy said trying to change the subject.

Jimmy held his hand up as if he had a knife and said. "Dunt, dunt, dunt…swinging his hand with a stabbing motion," they all started running. "Stop it Jimmy, I mean it!" Tommy yelled.

"Oh alright, let's go get some ice cream. I was trying to lighten things up a bit." Jimmy said.

They all sat together in a booth at the café and waited for their server so they could order. The server came over to their table. Sarah looked up and what she saw was sheer delight. There, standing before her was the dreamiest guy she had ever seen. He was tall, dark and handsome. He looked straight into Sarah's blue eyes and said, "Hi, I'm Nick. What can I get for you, miss?" His smile captivated her and she couldn't help but stare. He had the cutest dimples and the blackest eyes the color of onyx. Coal black curls framed his face. He was a young man of color. Sarah couldn't breathe nor could she speak.

"Hello, Sarah, Lotto?" Jimmy snapped his fingers.

Sarah jumped. "What? Oh! I'll have a root beer float." She was finally able to say.

Beth looked at Sarah then at the server. "Oh geez, she's got it bad."

Jimmy glared at the server and said, "Yeah, make that four and hurry up would ya, boy?"

Ignoring Jimmy's remark the server leaned over the table and said, "Would you like anything else miss?" Not waiting for a response he said, "Hey aren't you the girl that sings the angel song?"

Sarah's heart skipped a beat. She blushed and then turned away.

Jimmy said, "That's none of your business." He clenched his fist, face red with anger.

"Jimmy that's rude." said Sarah.

She looked at Nick and said, "Yes I am."

Nick smiled and said, "I thought so. I'll have your order right out to you." Then he gave her a wink.

Jimmy was fuming. "I'll knock his teeth down his throat. He has no business talking to you. Who does he think he is anyway?"

Tommy said, "Come on man he's harmless." Jimmy ran his hand through his hair and said, "Yeah you're right." Calming down he sat back and took a deep breath. Sarah and Beth looked at each other and read each other's thoughts. "What a hunk." They melted back in their seats dreamily and sighed.

Jimmy and Tommy both said in unison, "Good grief!"

The next day sitting in Sunday school the girls were whispering. Beth said, "His name is Nick Williams, he's seventeen and a straight A student. And get this his, dad owns the grocery store. That's all I could find out about him on short notice. So what do ya think Sarah?" Beth waited anxiously for Sarah to answer.

"What do you mean Beth? He wouldn't give me the time of day." Sarah said trying not to sound too interested.

"Well he sure gave you the time of day yesterday." Beth said teasingly.

"I've never seen Jimmy so intimidated." Beth said looking down at her bible. "You'd think he likes you or something." She snickered.

Miss Rose, the Sunday school teacher said, "Turn to Matthew 24 verses 4-8."

"We'll talk about it after church Beth let's listen to the lesson I want to hear this." Sarah whispered.

"OK, Sarah." Beth said as she sat back in her chair.

Sarah flipped through her bible to the passage.

And Jesus answered and said unto them, Take heed that no man deceive you. 5 For many shall come in my name, saying, I am Christ; and shall deceive many. 6 And ye shall hear of wars and rumors of wars: see that ye be not troubled: for all these things must come to pass, but the end is not yet. 7 For nation shall rise against nation, and kingdom against kingdom: and there shall be famines, and pestilences, and earthquakes, in divers places. 8 All these are the beginning of sorrows. (Matthew 24: 4-8

Looking at the Miss Rose asked, "What do you think Jesus meant when he said all these are the beginning of sorrows?"

Sitting in the back of the room was Nick Williams. He raised his hand stood up and said, "Miss Rose in the last days many things will take place like wars and famines and a lot of people will do terrible things, but Jesus said this isn't the end yet but it will be the beginning of sorrows. Everyone turned to look at him.

"Very good Nick," Miss Rose said. "I see you know your bible." She was very impressed. Rose was a woman of forty. She'd lived in Cedar Bluff for ten years. She was originally from Ohio and had never married. She sometimes sensed the prejudice against her being a Yankee and a woman. She understood all too well the hurt that prejudice can bring. But Jesus saved her when she was sixteen and she loved the Lord with all her heart. She didn't let things like color interfere with how she treated others. Black, white, yellow, red made no difference to her. She truly had the love of God in her heart. And the kids could feel that love and they respected her for her stand. It took Rose a very long time to be accepted into the congregation the "clique" was hard to win over but time and showing the love of God won the battle. Although some still gossiped and didn't want her on any of their committees. Thank the Lord the pastor was a real man of God and didn't listen to idle gossip.

"Yes ma'am." Nick said. "My daddy taught us to read our bible every night before we go to bed." Nick nodded as he sat back down. Nick wasn't afraid of what people thought of him he was taught to have respect for others and to never hang his head but to speak with confidence and authority. His daddy told him people might not like his color but they'd respect him. He taught him to stand tall, yet humble.

The girls sat up in utter surprise when they heard Nick speak up. They stared in shock and whispered to each other! "He goes to our church?" Nick saw the girls and gave a slight smile!

After church Sarah rushed into the living room, "Granny you'll never guess what happened in Sunday school. Remember I told you about Nick Williams? Well he goes to our church." Before Sarah could finish she saw Granny standing in the middle of the room.

"Sarah there's someone here to meet you." Granny said in a solemn voice.

Sarah stopped in mid-sentence…"Wha…." Before she could finish the word she stopped and stared then slowly closed her mouth.

"Hello Sarah I'm your grandmother, Beulah Todd. I've wanted to meet you for a very long time but many things got in my way. I hope you can forgive me." Mrs. Todd was very humble and had a kind demeanor. She was slender and sat very straight. Her skin was smooth and flawless it was the color of caramel and when she spoke wisdom radiated from her dark brown eyes. Streaks of silver ran through her hair which was wound tightly in a bun. She was regal, the light of the Lord shown on her countenance, she was humble yet confident a no nonsense personality.

Sarah ran to the woman threw her arms around her and without restraint hugged her and cried uncontrollably.

When the emotional landslide subsided they all composed themselves and sat down to have a long talk.

After a pause Sarah cleared her throat and asked. "What may I call you?"

Beulah looked at Norma Jean questioningly then said, "Well, my other grandkids call me Grandma B. That's what you may call me."

"Grandma B, I like that." Sarah said as she smiled then relaxed.

"I thought I needed to finally come see the famous young lady that sings like an angel and shares God's word with the lost. And also to tell you that Nick Williams is your cousin. Your father and Nick's mother, were brother and sister. Nick has been talking a lot about you ever since you came into the store I figured you were the one he was talking about. I told him all about you and I wanted to come meet you in person to let you know as well." Grandma B said, with tears in her eyes.

"Your father, David was a good man, he didn't deserve what was done to him but the Good Lord knows the reasons why things happen in a Christian's life. Your mama was a good girl too. I met her a few times. You have her eyes, but you have your daddy's smile and music ability. I can see that you have been taught right from wrong and that you are using your talent for the Lord." Grandma B clasped her hands together giving thanks to the Lord.

Sarah looked at Granny then at Grandma B "Yes ma'am Granny has taught me ever since I can remember that God is just and merciful and that we are to forgive if we want to be forgiven. I've had lots of questions about who I am and where I belong. There are lots of cruel people in the world. I try not to think about the ignorance I see. It's difficult for me; I don't seem to fit in anywhere. I …I… don't understand sometimes." Sarah said with a faraway look on her face.

Sarah looked down at her hands folded in her lap and then said, "Grandma B, I'm glad you came here today. Nick is very handsome. I'm glad you told me he's my cousin that explains the attraction I guess. I'd like to get to know my daddy's family if that's alright with ya'll. I feel like part of me has been missing all my life." Sarah looked at her Grandma B with love and compassion.

"Yes, child we've missed you too. Your daddy was going to be a missionary but he fell in love with your mama, and then someone took his life. I can see the call on your life is strong. God has already used you in such a mighty way. Don't let anything or anyone stop that flow. You have a long life ahead of you. You finish school and get your music degree. Fame is not what it's cracked up to be. There are too many pitfalls in that way of life." Grandma B said with conviction in her voice and in her eyes.

"You see Sarah, your great-great-grandfather was brought here from Africa he was King of his tribe. His name was Melique, (pronounced Ma-leek) which means King. The slave traders kidnapped him and sold him to the highest bidder. They sold his sons; ages two, five, eight, and ten and his daughter who was thirteen. They also kidnapped his wife, Amina who was pregnant, and later had a son. But they kept them together with Melique as house slaves. The only thing we know about his children is that after the slave action they were split up and sent to different parts of the south. They never saw each other again. Fortunately Melique's owners were good and kind people, they were Christians. They educated, taught him to read and do his numbers and they taught him about the true King Jesus.

Melique was intelligent and learned quickly. Through the years his master respected and counted on him to run his business. Mr. Williams was a man of integrity and strong moral character; when he was on his death bed he deeded the grocery store and land to Melique. Slaves weren't allowed to own land at that time. He wrote a letter to his attorney and stated that he was giving Melique and his wife and his three children that were born on his plantation, their freedom. The good Lord watched over Melique's children and somehow always made sure honest men took care of Mr. William's affairs. Even to this day. No one can take the land from us. It was to be our legacy handed down from generation to generation.

"Oh my goodness I had no idea. Thank you for sharing that with me it fills in so many gaps in my mind." Sarah was humbled and amazed at this news.

"All I've ever wanted was for God to be glorified." Sarah said. "I see now that God has been with me all my life because of the blessing of my great-great grandfather. The gift of my music is from a long line of intelligent and gifted people; if God wants to use it for His glory than I am more than willing. You're so right about fame; I only want what God wants. He showed me that He could touch a lot more people with one record then I could by myself. Mr. Berry, he's the producer of the record company, knew where I stood from the beginning. We made a deal." Sarah was firm and confident as she spoke to her grandmother.

"That's good to hear Sarah." Grandma B said, understanding what was in her granddaughter's heart.

Sarah had lots of questions as she continued to talk to her grandmother. "I guess the temptation was too strong for mama and daddy. They must have loved each other very much. Ignorance, jealousy and fear brought about his murder. Daddy never even knew about me. There are always consequences for sin. I'm not saying God caused my mama to die…" Sarah's eyes filled with tears her heart raced. She licked her lips and said, "I think about what would have happened if they had lived. That might have been even worse because of prejudice. I guess I'll never know." Sarah said reaching up and wiping tears from her face.

Granny had been silent while the two of them talked to each other, then she reached out and took Sarah's hand and said. "Sarah honey I didn't realize you had all these questions. I just didn't think about it. But I'm glad you finally got to meet the other side of your family. Maybe now some of those questions are answered. I've been meaning to tell you something for a long time Sarah and I guess now, is as good a time as any. You have Hebrew blood from our side of the family. Why back there in ancient times, you have relatives that can be traced to a disciple of Jesus. They were just ordinary men not one of the original men was a scholar or famous. But they were men God had picked for his purpose. And now he's chosen you as well. I believe the disciple was Timothy. I'll show you the genealogy later."

Sarah's eyes got huge as she took in a deep breath and said, "REALLY?"

Granny looked at Beulah who was smiling and nodded pleased at such news. Granny looked at Sarah and said, "Yes honey, really. I have it all documented in a book in my cedar chest. I've been meaning to tell you then remembered when Beulah was talking. I'll show it to ya'll later."

"That would be swell Granny." Sarah said still surprised at the news. "I can't believe it. I have Hebrew blood in my veins and royal blood too! Sarah was trying to absorb the news. Wait til Beth hears about this, I really am a princess." She thought to herself.

"So Beulah what do you think about our girl? Is she what you expected?" Granny asked?

"She's that and more. Beulah said. "I wonder if you'll do me a favor Sarah." Beulah was so proud of her granddaughter she couldn't leave without hearing her sing the angel song.

"Anything, Grandma B. what is it?" Sarah asked with love and respect in her heart for her Grandmother.

"Could you sing me the angel song?" Beulah said taking a deep breath and taking Sarah's other hand.

"Of course, I'd be happy too." Sarah squeezed Grandma B's hand and went to the piano.

Tears ran down her grandmother's face in a steady stream she could not control the emotion she felt listening to her granddaughter sing with such anointing. Years came crashing back as she thought about David. It had been too traumatic when her son

160

was murdered to get involved in her granddaughters life. She had missed out on seeing Sarah grow up. She decided right then that she'd never leave her again. And so Beulah lifted her voice and began to sing the angel song along with Sarah. Her voice was pure and rich it was a perfect tone. Sarah's eyes widened and her heart leapt as she listened to the melody that flowed from this woman whom she had longed to meet for so many years. Granny was crying too! This encounter was ordained by God an answered prayer for Sarah and her Grandma B.

When the song ended Granny said, "Well, we now know where Sarah gets her talent. That was beautiful Beulah." Granny wiped tears from her eyes. "We'll have to get together more often. How about coming over for dinner next week?" Granny asked hopefully.

"I'd like that Norma Jean." Beulah said as she stood to go. "Call me and let me know what's best for you."

"I sure will." Granny said feeling relieved and thankful Sarah had finally met her other grandma. "Maybe now she could go forward in her life." Granny thought.

Sarah looked with expectancy and thought. "Will I really see you again? Oh please say yes."

Beulah looked at Sarah as if reading her mind and said. "Sarah, I'm never letting you go again. You're my girl, my granddaughter blue eyes and all. Your daddy would be so proud of you." They hugged each other never wanting to let go.

Then Sarah said, "I love you Grandma B."

"I love you too sweet pea." Grandma B said and then added. "I'll be looking forward to your call for dinner next week Norma Jean."

A knock came at the door. It was Grandma B's ride.

"I'll call you, Beulah," Granny said hugging her good-bye.

The following week Grandma B was invited to dinner where they all had a lovely time. Nick, Beth, Tommy and Jimmy were also there. The family became closer as time went by. The holidays were shared with turkey dinners, collard greens, stuffing and black eyed peas and especially lots of love. There was lots of laughter, joy and good times, until one night. Everyone was sitting at the dinner table when they heard gun shots. Then a ball of fire came through the kitchen window. Everyone screamed. Uncle George grabbed a pitcher of water and doused the flame. Cars were doing donuts in the front yard and voices were yelling obscenities. Taffy was barking, glass shattered, and the sound of cars drove away as a police car pulled up in the yard.

George and the boys ran out the front door. George yelled, "Norma Jean you girls stay in the house."

It was the kid's senior year of high school and they would be graduating soon. Sheriff Dixon got out of the car and said, "George we heard there was going to be trouble at your place so I came over to check it out. It looks like they did a bit of damage to your place. Is anyone hurt?"

162

"We're all fine. This is unbelievable. We've never experienced this much trouble. Everyone has always gotten along just fine. Do you know who it was?" George asked.

"We have a pretty good idea. With graduation right around the corner kids get restless. Come on I'll help you write out a report," Sheriff Dixon said, assessing the situation he shook his head and said, "Things seem to be getting worse and probably will before it's all over. All I can say is we're doing the best with we can."

The night air was charged with the smell of smoke. Granny, Sarah and Beth waited inside until everything was clear. Then they went outside to see the damage. "Girls we're gona have to do a lot more praying." Granny said as she looked around the yard at all the mess. "Who in the world would do such a thing? Just look at my roses." Granny said feeling devastated by the destruction she saw before her. All the love and work she had put into her flowers gone in just a few minutes. She wanted to cry, scream, slap someone but there was no one around for her retaliation. She simply prayed silently even though she was angry. "Lord, please help me to forgive these…these…barbarians, because when I get my hands on them they'll wish they'd never ran over an old lady's roses." She fought back the tears that now ran freely down her cheeks.

"Oh Granny," Sarah said. She grabbed her grandmother and held tight; her body shook uncontrollably.

Granny tried to compose herself. She wiped her eyes and nose and tried to speak. In short breaths she said,

"I…am…just…so…angry! Look at my little concrete chicks and duck" she tried to say then she cried even harder.

Sarah not knowing what to say and broken up seeing Granny in such a state said, "I'll call Miss Rose in the morning so she can address this in Sunday school. She has a big influence on the high school kids; they look up to her and respect her."

"Thank you honey," Granny said as she stopped crying. "That will be a big help. I know I shouldn't react in such a fashion but it just got to me. I'm fine now. I can plant more roses. It's just so over whelming. I'm gona pray that God will get ahold of them and turn them every which way but loose."

The boys began to pick up some of the debris.

Tommy said, "Granny I know we're supposed to return good for evil but this really makes me mad."

"Yeah me too," said Jimmy. "If I find out who did this, I'll turn them every which way but loose."

As Nick lifted a log off the ground he said, "And I'll help you, Jimmy."

"Boys I appreciate that but God says, vengeance is mine." Granny said. "It's a terrible thing to fall into the hands of an angry God. He'll get 'em, just watch and see."

A week later sheriff Dixon knocked on the door. "Hi George, I came by to tell you we caught those boys who vandalized your property."

Granny came and stood behind George and listened.

"What happened sheriff?" George asked.

164

Looking at George with pride in his voice he said, "There was a chase out on highway 10…the boy's car went over the bridge with them inside. No one got hurt. But Ted, Larry and Dale Hobson were stuck in the car when it began to sink into the lake. The officer on site dove in after them. He said it was the craziest thing. All three boys were terrified as they yelled; "Help…Help…Jesus, save us! We're sorry for tearing up Granny Evan's yard, don't let us die! We'll change our evil ways!"

Granny stood there, laughed and thought to herself, as she listened to the sheriff, "Serves them boys right doing what they did, thank you Jesus for teaching them a lesson."

"They'll be by next week to clean up the damages they caused." The sheriff said as he chuckled. "They should have never messed with Granny she's got a pipeline to heaven. The Good Lord won't put up with that."

"Thank you sheriff that'll be fine I'll be expecting them," said George reaching out to shake the sheriff's hand.

"Oh and by the way, they'll all be in church on Sunday." The sheriff said laughing as he shook George's hand, and turned to walk away.

The Graduation

Return, O Lord, how long? And let it repent thee concerning thy servants. Psalm 90:13

Two months left until graduation. People were discontented and a little fearful of what was coming. Times were changing the world was going in a whole new direction. Martin Luther King had made a speech, "I have a Dream." From taxies to water fountains, buses, to public restrooms and Mom and Pop cafes the white man's kingdoms were coming down, the coloreds were making a stand. They no longer accepted the signs that read for 'WHITE'S ONLY'. Change was here and there was no going back. Years of segregation was coming to a close. Integration was here to stay. There would always be racial differences but respect for others rights was a fight they would someday win. And that someday was at hand! It was time to stand up for their freedom.

What would the world hold for Sarah and Beth, Tommy, and Jimmy and Nick? Only time would tell.

As Valedictorian, Nick would give a speech for their senior class. His outstanding academic achievement and community service helped win over the majority of the neighborhood regardless of race. But there were still many who did not approve of a colored boy being the leader of their senior class. One night, white robed men paid the Williams family a visit. They threw rocks in the store window, and a large cross was set on fire in their front lawn. Sarah was stalked and harassed even more than before. The next morning she went to feed Taffy but couldn't find her.

Sarah called out, "Taffy, come on girl it's time for breakfast." But Taffy didn't come. Sarah went to the back yard and kept calling, "Taffy come on girl." Then she spotted her lying half way inside the dog house. As she got closer she saw blood. She gasped, ran to Taffy's side, and pulled the cherished dog to her chest hugging her tight. She buried her face in the dogs fur as she sobbed uncontrollably then great sobs followed that turned into wailing. "Why? Why? Why would anyone do this? She was a good dog the best friend I'd ever known." Sarah screamed. "Why do they hate me so much? Why have they taken my best friend from me?" Sarah screamed clutching onto Taffy with all her might she was devastated.

Granny and Uncle George ran out back to see what had happened. They ran towards the dog house. When they got to Sarah they were horror struck. They fell down beside her and cried as well. Sarah looked up at Uncle George, grief stricken with questions in her eyes. Granny tried to console her, "Sarah, come on child let George take care of this." But Sarah would not budge she clung to Taffy. Then Uncle George said, "Sarah let's put her to rest in a peaceful place." He picked Taffy up and carried her around to the front of the house. He told Granny to bring him a sheet. He went to get a shovel. Sarah sat with blood stains on her clothes and sobbed. Nothing would ever be the same again. Taffy was gone.

After a while they all gathered at a small grave in the front yard next to the oak tree. They said their goodbyes and waited as Sarah sang. Then she prayed.

"Lord Jesus, Taffy was a sweet, loving dog and I loved her she was my very best friend. Please make sure she has lots of friends in heaven to play with. And a stick to play fetch. She loves music too Lord. And tell her I'll see her again one day. Thank you Jesus amen."

It was a difficult time for everyone. Losing Taffy was a horrible blow and it would take a long time for that hurt to heal.

Beth, Tommy and Jimmy were labeled Negro lovers but it didn't stop them from standing up for what they knew was right.

It was finally graduation day. It should have been a time for celebration but instead it was a dark time for everyone. Maybe in the future things would be better but right now people were leery of what every day would bring.

As Nick gave his speech Tommy and Jimmy stood on stage behind him to protect him. They had become very good friends especially when Jimmy found out he was Sarah's cousin and not a potential rival. Sarah and Beth also stood watch. Most of the senior class supported Nick; after all they had voted him in as senior class president. Nick had a way with people, a quick wit and charming smile. Nick's dynamic way with words could win anyone over. He loved God and was constantly serving others. There were a few hecklers in the crowd.

But as Nick stood to speak the entire auditorium grew silent. *"My fellow classmates, teachers, administrators, staff, friends and family; President Lincoln once said, and I quote, (Freedom is not the right to do what we want, but what we ought. Let us have faith that right makes might and in that faith let us, to the end, dare to do our duty as we understand it.)*

"Times are changing, and I believe for the better even though they are terrifying and rocky. We are the future, we are the ones who will make the difference in our world and if we don't stand for what is right and if we don't let our voices be heard then evil men will win. Stand for truth; stand for justice, stand and do not back up for anything or anyone. It's our time, it's our duty as citizens of any race; white, black, red, yellow it's not the color of the skin that matters it's what's in your heart! You set the example and when we look back on these far distant days, "the good old days," we will be proud that we stood for what is right!" There will be a day when "race" will be just a four letter word. People will let go of ignorance and fear and then the human race will begin to grow, but without God in the center of our lives there will be no hope. So this is what I say to you all, when you look at another human being look past the color of their skin and see the real person. Understand we all need each other. And as President Lincoln said, "Let us have faith that right makes might and in that faith let us, to the end, dare

to do our duty as we understand it." Stick together class of 1963, *and make the world a better place to live for our children and our children's children."*

Nick's voice rose in a charismatic triumphant blast of, *"Freedom is not free; it takes hard, determined, work and dedication and even sometimes it can take our very lives. With men it is impossible but with God ALL things are possible."*

The audience went wild; they were moved by Nick's words even those who opposed him because of prejudice. Everyone stood and cheered for this amazing young man as he threw his graduation cap into the air. The whole *"Class of 1963"* shouted and threw their caps into the air too. They looked past color and at that moment there were united they were one.

After the ceremony Jimmy, Tommy, Beth, Sarah and Nick went over to Sarah's house where Granny and Uncle George were serving cake and punch. Some of their other class mates were there as well. They played records and danced. At midnight everything settled down. Bobby Vinton's record was playing on the record player; most everyone was slow dancing to his song B*lue Velvet.* Jimmy was dancing with Sarah. It was obvious that Jimmy was smitten with Sarah and had been for a very long time.

"Hey Lotto, you wanna know something?" Jimmy whispered in Sarah's ear.

"What's that?" Sarah asked dreamily.

"I'm gonna miss you. We'll be miles apart, I don't know if I can take it or not." Jimmy tightened his arm around her.

"I know Jimmy, it's kind of scary but I believe it's where God wants me. It's only for four years. My contract will be up and then who knows." Sarah was lost in the song as they swayed back and forth she felt as if she were a thousand miles away. She didn't want the song to end.

"Sarah, you know I love you don't you?" Jimmy finally confessed.

Sarah's heart raced wildly, as she said, "What? I had no idea I figured we were really good friends I mean, we all grew up together. You were always making fun of me."

"That's because I liked you so much. I never knew what to say so I covered it up by calling you names." Jimmy said feeling a little embarrassed, not sure what to say next.

Sarah stopped dancing and looked at him she didn't know what to say. "I always liked you Jimmy, I liked you a lot. But I never thought about love. My heart and mind have always been on my singing and music serving God and helping people. And well, you know, my skin is different than yours. I didn't want to cause any problems."

Jimmy sighed. "I must have misread the signals. And for the record I never thought about the color of your skin. I've always admired your bravery. You were the coolest girl in the whole school." Jimmy felt rejected and hurt.

"What signals?" Sarah was dumbfounded.

"Never mind Sarah, I understand forget I said anything. I'm going to law school and you have your calling, it's just not meant to be. Forget it OK? I have to go." Jimmy kissed her on the cheek and left in a hurry. His heart was breaking. He didn't want her to see the tears.

Beth walked over to Sarah. "What was that all about, as if I didn't already know?"

"What do you mean Beth? Have I been that oblivious to everything going on around me? I had no clue Jimmy felt that way." Sarah had tears in her eyes. "I wouldn't hurt him for anything in the world. I didn't realize." Sarah ran to her room sobbing.

"Well I guess I gotta go too. I'll call you tomorrow Beth. Tell Sarah not to be too hard on herself, Jimmy will be here tomorrow I'm sure and straighten everything out. See ya later Freckles." Tommy said.

"Hey Nick you want a lift home?" Tommy asked.

"You bet." said Nick. "I came over with Jimmy but he left in a hurry."

"Yeah he and lotto had a mix-up I guess. They'll get it worked out tomorrow I'm sure." Tommy said opening the screen door, Nick followed as the boys left for home.

Beth was spending the night with Sarah. Entering Sarah's bedroom she heard her crying. Beth spoke lightly, "Sarah what's wrong?"

"Oh Beth I've messed up everything. I knew Jimmy loved me but I didn't want to admit it to myself or to him. I didn't want to hurt him but I know I did. I pretended I didn't love him because I thought it would displease the Lord." Sarah said trying to figure out what to do next, crying she said, "What should I do? He'll never talk to me again."

"Sarah, Jimmy understands about that, but you should have told him the truth." Beth said with disappointment in her voice and a look of distress.

"I'm afraid." Sarah said. "If I tell him, he'll wait for me and I don't want him to be wasting his time. I don't know what the future is going to bring." Sarah's heart was breaking she ran her hand through her hair exasperated, trying to think how she could make this right.

"None of us know what the future holds Sarah. Where's the girl of faith I know and admire, the girl who's always strong and confident, the girl who always knows exactly what she wants and what to say." Beth said breathlessly, trying to get through to her best friend.

Catching her breath, Beth put her arm around her friend and hugged her. "Tomorrow you can call Jimmy and let him know how you really feel. Don't think about it, do it!" Beth said flashing her green eyes at Sarah. She knew that look and knew Beth meant business when she made that face. It was like looking into the eyes of a green eyed monster it sent fear straight to your heart.

"OK Beth," but as Sarah was finishing her sentence a shiver ran through her body and Jimmy's smile flashed through her mind.

Beth held onto her and said, "Are you sure you're alright Lotto?"

"Yes, I guess so. I just had a vision of Jimmy; he smiled and walked away into the bright light, it was all around him. That's so strange." Sarah said. "I'll call him first thing in the morning and tell him the truth."

Jimmy couldn't stop thinking about Sarah and what a fool he had made of himself as he drove home. "I know she feels the same way. All the signals were there. I couldn't have been wrong. I'll call her tomorrow and get everything straightened out." Jimmy thought. He reached to turn on the radio and was pushing buttons to find a station. It was just a split second; he saw something fly across the road in front of him it was black and sinister looking. "What was that?" He thought. Then as he was making his turn around the curve he hit a slick spot. The car started to swerve; he could not get control. The car flipped over and over and over, six times then came to a halt, hitting a tree. Jimmy's head hit the steering wheel and flung back against the seat. Glass shattered and dug into his face and arms. Blood was pouring from his head. The impact had knocked him out for a moment. Head hanging forward and stunned he rolled his head around and began to realize what had happened. Moaning he tried to move but his foot was stuck between the door and the seat, the pain was unbearable. He tried to focus; the car was on fire, he smelled gas. Then Ca-Boom the car exploded Jimmy's last thoughts were … "Jesus tell Lotto I love her."

Jimmy's guardian angel *Sage* tried everything to get Jimmy's attention but he was so distracted by the *demons of condemnation and humiliation* taunting him that *he* couldn't get through. Then the spirit of *death* flew in front of his car. There was nothing *Sage* could do but hold him as he took his final breath.

Sarah and Beth were eating breakfast when the phone rang. It was Jimmy's mother.

"Hello. Yes this is Sarah."

"Sarah, this is Mrs. Stevens, Jimmy's mother. I have some bad news. I don't know any other way to say this. There was an accident last night, sobs came between words…" It took all the strength she could muster to say the words, *"Sarah, Jimmy is dead!"*

Sarah stood frozen she dropped the phone and screamed, "No!!!!!! Oh God! No!" Sarah dropped to the floor in hysterics. She screamed, "I have to tell him, I have to tell him something…he can't be dead!" Guilt gripped Sarah as she sobbed uncontrollably.

Granny came running in to see what was wrong. The phone was dangling from the table. She picked it up and said, "Hello this is Norma Jean who is this?" She heard sobs on the other end of the phone. "This is Jimmy's mother. Jimmy was driving home last night and lost control of his car. The police and fire department rushed to the scene and found the car totally burned up and," she couldn't finish her sentence…I'm sorry Norma Jean I'll have to explain it later, I, sobbing… she said I have to…go."

Beth not knowing what to think looked at Sarah, "What's wrong? What happened? Who's dead?"

Sarah looked at Beth and screamed, "Jimmy, Jimmy's dead!"

Beth broke into tears, threw her arms around Sarah and they both sobbed. The next few days were agony as they waited for the funeral.

During the service' Sarah was numb. She couldn't bear the thought that she would never get the chance to tell Jimmy how she really felt. Her heart was broken. Beth and Nick sang, Amazing Grace. Tommy held onto Sarah as she wept. "Why…why did this have to happen? Jimmy…Oh Jimmy." Sarah moaned with grief.

The pastor read *Psalm 23*. *"The Lord is my shepherd I shall not want…He maketh me to lie down in green pastures…He restores my soul…*

Nick got up to do the eulogy. "Jimmy was one of a kind, he was my best friend and I will miss him. We can't bring him back but we can be with him again someday. Only God knows that day and hour. Jimmy has gone too soon yet if he were standing here right now he'd say, don't cry for me I'm in a wonderful place. I know you will miss me but it's OK everything is as it should be."

Sarah shook trying to be strong but she could not stop crying. Beth held onto her and cried as well. As Nick finished talking Beth said, "Sarah, I know you'll want to be alone with Jimmy, I'll see ya back at the house." Beth held a handkerchief out to Sarah so she could wipe her eyes. Beth, sniffled, wiped her eyes and said, "I'm so sorry sweet friend, I'm so very sorry."

Sarah fell upon the grave and wept uncontrollably until there were no more tears. Then she said, "Jimmy, Oh Jimmy. I'm so sorry if I'd only known. If I would have just said I love you back, none of this would have happened. How will I ever be able to get over this? I never will." She heard a small voice within her say. "Sing the angel song for me Lotto." *Sage* stood nearby watching Sarah.

Sage whispered to her, "Jimmy loves you Sarah; he's with the Father, you don't have to grieve as one who has no hope."

"Jimmy? Is that you?" Sarah pulled herself up from the ground and looked around. There was no one there. She cleared her throat. Then she held her face towards the sky and began to sing…

Though times are hard
I'm by your side
Your tears I hold within my hand
No matter what I'll hold you close
Look to the one who understands.
Though fear may come, and tears may fall
Be still and know, that I am God
Let perfect peace restore your heart
And know my love we'll never part

Chorus:
I walked the road of trials and torment
I sat with those who love me still
But on the cross
I felt the suffering of all the ones who love me most.
The birds they sing a nightly chorus
Of joy and peace to all they bring
So lift your voice and head toward heaven

And learn their song, their song and sing.

He gives me peace, He gives me life, the angels sing be
glorified

Praise to the King our mighty King

We're going home on angels wings.

When in the stillness now at midnight

I see the star of love so bright

I'll never ever doubt my Savior

For He will lead me through the night

And on the breeze I hear Him whisper…

Press on my child and do not weep

For at the dawn you'll have your answer

So close your eyes and go to sleep.

Chorus:

I walked the road of trials and torment

I sat with those who love me still

But on the cross

I felt the suffering of all the ones who loved me most.

The birds they sing a nightly chorus

Of joy and peace to all they bring

So lift your voice and head toward heaven

And learn their song, their song and sing.

He gives me peace, He gives me life, the angels sing be
glorified

Praise to the King our mighty King
We're going home on angels wings.

I wake at dawn and have my answer
His peace I sing to all who wait
And then He gives me sweet assurance
I'll never, ever be alone
These souls I bring to heaven's harvest
They are the ones who overcome
And now my love
You have your answer
Your journey's only just begun!

"I love you Jimmy. I'm sorry I didn't tell you but I was afraid. Please forgive me." Sarah said with renewed strength.

"I'm making you a promise from now on I'll say what's in my heart with conviction and truth. I'll never be afraid again." She felt numb and incomplete but she had hope and faith that this was not the end. A cool breeze brushed her cheek, a bird sang in a nearby tree then peace that passed all understanding flooded her heart and soul. She knew Jimmy had kissed her good-bye.

"I'll see ya around Lotto." She sensed him say. But it was *Sage* giving her a message from Jimmy. He then left her knowing that her guardian angel Philomel, which means, the nightingale, would be guarding her closely.

Sarah still couldn't eat, she couldn't sleep. All she could remember was the night Jimmy left after telling her he loved her. The look on his face waiting to hear those four precious words, *I love you too*, but he never did. The guilt she felt hung around her heart with a death grip and she could not get a release.

The demons of shame, self-pity, and guilt laughed in a disgusting guttural sound. "We've got her now she'll never recover. We'll make her life a miserable mess of self-doubt, guilt and loathing. She'll never be happy again. The demons were proud of how well their job was going.

Philomel stood watch over Sarah hovering close so that the demons couldn't get closer to her. Then they heard someone praying.

"No!" Shrieked the demonic beasts, "not the praying"....they clutched their pointy ears and made a mad dash for cover, then flew out of the room.

Granny was in her bedroom praying. *"Lord Jesus, protect my granddaughter she's been hurt terribly. Jesus I know the call that's on her life please don't let this discourage her. Bring her through this and make her stronger. Help her to see that even though Jimmy is gone to heaven that she still has a work to do here. I bind every hindering spirit and cast them far away from her. Thank you Jesus, now please give her a peaceful sleep. Amen."*

Sarah drifted into a deep sleep and had a dream. Jimmy came to her and held something out to her. It was a little golden box engraved with two angels. Sarah opened the box and what she heard filled her with joy and peace. A rich baritone voice sang this song.

Tell Them You Love Them

His loving words ring in my ear
As he professed his love for me
Not knowing then, his life would end
Leaving behind his dearest friend
Oh wait, oh wait…
Please do not go; I have to say, I love you so
I was afraid, to let you know; and now it is too late
Listen to me, all you who say
I'll put it off, for one more day
That day will end; and you won't know

So tell them now; before they go
Oh how I love you…I'll always love you
I hope you understand
I was afraid, fear gripped my heart
Leaving us broken and torn apart
Taken from me in the night
Life for me will never be the same
Because you're not here; when I call your name
I love you now, I always will
His words came back to me,
Be still my nightingale, I understand

The love I gave will set you free

Don't let your love be hidden from me

Sing out Sarah and for all to hear

True love will always conquer fear

Sing my bright star, be strong and true

Love will protect and rescue you

The love I give is from above

So when you sing, my precious dove

Let love bring comfort to all who hear

Surrender your life as I call to thee

Love's gracious gift will set you free

Lift high your voice and sing today

Don't hold back, sing and obey

True love will conquer every fear

He's wiped away every tear

My shattered dreams and broken heart

Now mended and repaired

"Sarah my love, do this for me

Lift high the banner for all to see

Sing Sarah, sing for me!"

Peace settled over Sarah's spirit and she slept soundly. She woke refreshed the next morning. But she was still not herself. She went to the kitchen to get a glass of milk. Sitting there she contemplated everything that had taken place over the last few weeks and thought she would lose her mind. She tried to pray but couldn't get through all she could do was think about Jimmy and the fact that he was gone.

In order to keep from going completely insane she told herself she'd tuck Jimmy's words deep within her heart and continue to do what God had called her to do. She wasn't exactly sure what that was, but she knew God would let her know when the time was right. "I know God wants me to sing. She thought. But God I don't feel like singing. Jesus I'm broken. I don't want to do anything." Tears came to her eyes again.

Being pulled from her inner thoughts she heard Granny say, "Sarah, I'm not sure you should be going to New York City right now. I don't like the idea of you being there all alone." Then she handed Sarah the newspaper.

Devastated by what was going on in her personal life she was unaware of what was happening in the world. Racial unrest and riots had broken out all over Alabama. African-Americans were tired of discrimination, and prejudice that still held them as slaves in the eyes of many. Now was the time to stand up for what was right. They would have justice and freedom. They were Americans too!

"But we've been planning this for two years." Sarah said as she held the Cedar Bluff Post newspaper in her hand. She looked at the headline on the front page it said, **"The Road to Civil Rights Getting to the March on Washington DC, August 28, 1963."**

Sarah's plan was to go to New York City, where for the next four years she would be completing her education in music. From there she'd be going to the mission field in South Africa. At least that's what Sarah thought, but God had other plans. As she read the article a light clicked on. She said, "I know what it is God wants me to do. I've got to go to Washington DC." She said with renewed strength and vision. "This is exactly what I needed. Sarah gave Granny a kiss on the cheek and reached for the phone but as she did it rang. It was Beth. "Sarah, I spoke to Tommy and Nick we've all decided to go to Washington DC to march. We talked about it and it's too important to pass up this opportunity. History is being made and we want to be a part of it." Beth said her voice almost in hysterics. "We want you." But before she could get the words out Sarah said, "Yes I know Beth; I was about to call you when the phone rang." Sarah said. "I read the newspaper article just now; about the march and you confirmed what God spoke to my heart. When do you want to leave?" Sarah asked.

"Tommy said he will drive his car, it will save time and money and it'll be safer than taking a bus." Beth said. "Can you be ready to leave by 6:00 in the morning? There's going to be a lot of people so we need to travel light." Beth was so excited she could hardly talk.

"Yes I can" said Sarah. "I need to let Granny and Uncle George know the change of plans. I'll see ya in the morning. Bye." Sarah hung up the phone.

Before Sarah could tell Granny the news, Granny was smiling and said, "I know honey, you do what you need to do. George and I will be praying for you." Sarah grabbed her grandmother and squeezed her tight not wanting to let go. Granny knew this was just the thing Sarah needed and she knew God would protect her girl.

"Granny will you do me a favor and call Grandma B and let her know what's going on as well. I don't want her to worry," Sarah said as she hurried to her room.

"Don't worry about that honey I'll let her know. You concentrate on getting ready and I'll call Beulah." Granny said.

"Thanks Granny." Sarah said from her room while she packed.

Granny got up to make the call. Beulah's phone rang, "Hello," said Beulah.

"Oh hello Norma Jean, you're calling to tell me that Sarah's going to the march in Washington DC? Do you think that's wise with all the riots going on in DC right now? Well if her mind is made up then, we need to pray real hard that the Lord will keep them safe. It's very frightening. Are you sure this is what she should do? Well, if Nick is going too they'll be in good hands. Alright I'll continue to pray. The good Lord will help us. Thank you for calling. Tell her I love her and I'll see her when she gets home. Bye Norma Jean. I love you too!"

A Day to Remember

Oh satisfy us early with thy mercy; that we may rejoice and be glad all our days. Psalm 90:14

As they arrived in Washington DC there was mayhem everywhere and yet no one was causing trouble. "I've never seen anything like this in my life." Sarah said as she looked at the line of buses parked all along the streets in the city. The sounds of horns blowing, and groups of people both black, and white, as well as other Americans who wanted change, were marching and singing, *"We Shall Overcome!"* There was a sort of quiet resolve it wasn't just about racism it was for the people, all people. Sarah felt freedom in her heart and wanted to stand for what she believed was right.

Tommy found a spot to park about a mile away from the Washington Monument. He turned to his three friends and said, "Thank goodness it's a miracle we found this parking spot. We're gona have to walk a ways but it should be pretty safe let's all stick close with all these people no telling what might happen."

They fell in with others as they walked together and all sang courageously. They were proud and brave, men and women marching, determined and on a mission. Carrying signs that read, "Government of ALL PEOPLE…FOR ALL THE PEOPLE ~ By ALL the PEOPLE;" "END SEGREGATION IN PUBLIC SCHOOLS;" "WE MARCH FOR JOBS FOR DECENT PAY NOW;" "WE DEMAND VOTING RIGHTS;" "WE MARCH TOGETHER: CATHOLIC, JEWS, PROTESTANTS!"

All of a sudden there was a disturbance and everyone started running. Policemen with sticks came out of nowhere and stopped a group of men that had swastika arm bands.

"Move along, move along." The cops shouted poking them with their clubs. They gathered the Nazi want-a-be's together, about ten of them, and subdued them before they could cause trouble and then a police van came and took them away.

"There must be over 200,000 people or more here today," Beth shouted as she struggled to get through the crowd. There was an ocean of people all in one accord. People were dressed in their Sunday best. Some sitting on the ground waiting and others just standing. They were proud and ready to be a part of this great march for freedom! Not quite sure what was going to take place they prayed silently, sang songs and believed change would come. They were moved with passion for a dream that was long overdue to come into fruition. It was past time for what was needed. Time for truth to come forth and by the hand of God they would make their dream come true.

Then Sarah spotted Mahalia Jackson on the platform. She became more determined than ever to get closer to the stage.

Mahalia Jackson, the Queen of Gospel Music; was her model and inspiration. Mahalia began to sing.

"Hurry we've got to get closer to the platform." Sarah pushed and shoved but the crowd was not moving.

Nick yelled, "Come on I see an opening, follow me. Sarah, hold my hand and don't let go."

Tommy grabbed Beth's hand and they inched their way as close to the stage as they could get.

Sarah stared in awe as she heard the music of an old soul pour over her very own soul and she wept. But they were tears of joy and fulfillment. "Oh, thank you God, for this beautiful lady, thank you that you allowed me to finally see and hear Mahalia." Sarah was beside herself with excitement and renewed strength. "Now I know I can do what you've called me to do with freedom and unending love and gratitude. Amen." This was Sarah's prayer.

As Mahalia finished her song the crowd roared with cheers and applause she didn't just sing a song she brought a Holy Ghost prayer meeting to the streets of the White House. Her song "How I Got Through," is an anthem for her people who have been oppressed, kidnapped from their country, whipped, enslaved, beaten, tortured and killed and now they want their freedom.

It was a new beginning for African-Americans; it was a turning point for all Americans. The battle was finally beginning to be won. There was still a long way to go but today was a victory that would not be deterred or forgotten.

It was an experience Sarah would carry with her for the rest of her life. It no longer mattered if she was white or black or mixed, she was a child of the Most High God and now she had purpose, and direction that would take her, to her destiny and fulfill the call that was on her life.

Tommy, Beth, Nick and Sarah were all changed that day. Tommy went on to receive his law degree and served in Washington DC as senator for Alabama. Sarah, Beth and Nick finished their degrees and were ready to start their ministries for the Lord.

Nick became a pastor in Tennessee. Beth went to Africa as a missionary. But Sarah didn't go to Africa as a missionary. Over the next few years Sarah went on tour as a gospel singer, part of the Mahalia Jackson music team. She experienced so many things on the tour. Mahalia was truly a wonderful lady full of the love of God and she taught Sarah that life was more than getting things; it was more important to spread the love of God and give him the very best you have to offer.

The place she most enjoyed was their trip to the Holy Land. Israel the place where Jesus lived, ministered to thousands; died, was buried and was raised to life from the grave. It was for all man kind of every race. Her favorite place was in the Garden of Gethsemane at the foot of the Mount of Olives in Jerusalem where Jesus prayed. She highlighted the passage in her bible. (Luke 22:40-44) King James Version

[40] And when he was at the place, he said unto them, pray that ye enter not into temptation.

⁴¹ And he was withdrawn from them about a stone's cast, and kneeled down, and prayed,

⁴² Saying, Father, if thou be willing, remove this cup from me: nevertheless not my will, but thine, be done.

⁴³ And there appeared an angel unto him from heaven, strengthening him.

⁴⁴ And being in an agony he prayed more earnestly: and his sweat was as it were great drops of blood falling down to the ground.

Each time she read this passage she could see Jesus in great agony pleading for his disciples to pray with him. But all they could do was sleep.

Sarah prayed, "Lord please help me, I never want to be asleep when you need me most."

Philomel stood by her liege as she heard her pray. Spreading her beautiful angel wings, of soft feathers over Sarah protecting her and filling her with the love of the Father she said, "Be blessed little song bird. You are blessing the Almighty."

Sarah got more than she ever dreamed possible not only a friend for life but an education that would open many doors for her. But there was one door she wanted to open and that was the door where God could use her most.

After completing the tour which was the dream of a lifetime she came home for a short rest. "Granny, I've been praying for the last two weeks and I believe God is leading me in another direction. I can never repay the magnificent blessing I've had over the last few years. I've been to Israel and walked in the Garden of Gethsemane where Jesus prayed. I saw over five-thousand souls give their lives to Jesus during our tour and after all, that's what the journey is about. Singing on tour with Mahalia and her team was amazing but now it's time for me to do something else. I've matured and I'm ready for the challenge." Sarah said as she sat at the kitchen table with her grandmother.

"Sarah, I have confidence in you and I know God does too. Whatever it is, you know he said he'd confirm his word to you. All you have to do is have faith." Granny picked up her coffee and took a sip. "Don't you worry, I know Jesus is working on your behalf and will give you the answers you need."

Uncle George came in the front door with the mail in his hand. Holding up a letter he read, *"Miss Sarah Evans.* Here Sarah looks like this one's for you."

Sarah looked up, took the letter and said, "Thanks Uncle George, speaking of confirmation, listen to this."
Dear Miss Sarah,

I know you remember me so I'm not going to beat around the bush. Years ago you came to our little country garage. Holly and Molly fixed a tar for your Uncle George. God used you in a mighty way that day and since that time we've grown into quite a large church. God moves in miraculous ways here. You're Cousin Nick is one of our Associate Pastors and has recommended you for a position here as the Director of Foreign missions. I want you to fast and pray about this Sarah. I know you are very busy traveling and ministering in music for the Lord. Pray, Sarah, and let me know if this is where the good Lord Jesus wants you to minister. I already have an idea but you need to know too.

Come check us out we'd love for you to come sing and minister as soon as you can. We'll talk about all the details when you arrive.

Here's some highlights of what's taken place over the years. I took some bible correspondence courses and found that I had a gift for learning. I picked things up quickly. Then God sent me three ministers from Bible College which helped start the church. Miraculously people flocked here, where they could feel love, and something different about all of us. Before we knew it, the whole town began to change. The gift of prophecy, helps, teachers, tongues and interpretation of tongues flowed. God's love multiplied. There were challenges with different denominations but as the church began to intercede and discern spirits we cast them out and everything began to fall into place. People took shifts praying around the clock. Seven days a week someone was in the church praying and reading God's word. A day care and school was established. Fund raisers were organized to help support the ministry. New converts were taught the word of God, and then they were filled with the Holy Spirit. He, the Holy Spirit distributed gifts to everyone. Hearts were humble and teachable. Everything flowed supernaturally. People were kind and loving and everyone pitched in to help wherever help was needed. The anointing was so great that even animals got along; and the farmland grew in abundance of fruits and vegetables there was peace and harmony that could not be explained other than it was God. Grocery stores donated food for the school. Banks donated money for supplies. Gas stations donated gas for the buses to run so that children could come to school every day, there was miracle after miracle. And now God is calling you Sarah. But you pray and let Him tell you. Then come visit us and see for yourself.

Love in Christ, your sister,

Matilda Rose "Matty"

"Granny, Uncle George you remember Molly and Holly, the twins who had the garage and fixed Uncle George's tires, when we were on our way to sing on the radio. I was ten years old, you know, when you and Beth and I were on our way to Tennessee? Well it says that a huge church came out of that encounter; they're asking me to come and sing at the church and want to offer me a position." Sarah had no idea how big the church had become. All she remembered was that God had touched these country folk years ago in a miraculous way. "I'm going to accept the invitation."

Granny and Uncle George looked at each other and grinned. George winked at Sarah, "I think that's a great idea. I know this is of God."

"Amen," Granny said. "I remember that trip when you came back you were a changed little girl. As I remember that's when you met Zeema. The last letter I got from her she said she had moved to Nashville. Sarah you go where the Spirit leads you and don't let anything or anyone hold you back."

"Alright Granny I won't. I'll be leaving next week." Sarah said with renewed energy.

Upon arriving at, *"Peace Like a River, Church of God,"* Sarah checked the address on the letter to make sure she was in the right place. "Yep it's the correct address. No garage, no broken down cars or dogs lying around. She drove around a half moon circular drive. Stain-glass windows of Jesus the shepherd, leading his sheep beside green pastures and quiet streams of water were the scenes in the glass. They were inlaid in the walls of the church from ground to roof, they were beautiful. "If this is the place, WOW this is impressive." She thought.

Two men in white suits stood in front of double oak doors and greeted each person as they entered and said, "Welcome, glad to see you this morn'n." They smiled as they shook everyone's hand.

As Sarah stepped out of the car and started up the walkway one of the men came out to greet her.

Sarah was wearing an ankle length; pink chiffon dress and white sling back shoes. Her hair hung loose below her shoulders; bushy as usual with a headband of pink to hold it back from her face. Her blue eyes sparkled as she shook the usher's hand. Her smile was always sincere and joyful causing everyone she met to feel her genuine spirit of grace and beauty but she never realized the affect she had on people. The love she had in her heart for God shown in her eyes making her almost glow. People automatically responded to the Spirit of God that radiated from her.

"Hello, glad to have you Miss Sarah, we've been expecting you. I'd recognize you anywhere. I've been a fan for years." The usher said. "You don't remember me I was a little boy the first time we met. But I'll never forget you. Because of the anointing on the angel song you sang, I've had an amazing life. I wanted to be the first one to welcome you here today and say thank you. My name is Tim, I'm Holly and Molly's cousin, but we can talk later. Maw is on the platform, I mean Sister Matilda Rose she goes by sister Matty. I'll usher you to the front."

Sarah entered the sanctuary and to her delight there were pink, yellow and red roses; golden sunflowers; blue and white hydrangeas and butterfly weed strategically placed on mahogany tables, in beautiful crystal and 19th century Imari vases throughout the huge room. The floors in the lobby were made out of Italian marble. As she looked up into the Cathedral ceilings she saw murals of angels painted there. Rows and rows of white pews were lined across the sanctuary even into the balcony where red carpets rolled out and up the stairs. Deep oak banisters surrounded the hand rails as they spiraled around and upward where hundreds of people were praising God, it was breathtaking. A choir of about 150 people stood on the platform they were dressed in purple and silver robes. Their voices rang out in a glorious gospel hymn. Violins, saxophones, piano, flutes and even a harp made a harmonious sound. Timpani kept time as the sounds of what sounded like heaven filled the air. Soprano's, alto's, tenors and baritone voices, flooded her with emotion that caused chills to run up and down her arms and made

195

the hair stand up on the back of her neck. Such energy, Sarah could hardly maintain her composure. She wanted to run and shout and sing and dance all at the same time. She began to twirl around praising God. Others joined in the worship it was not unusual in the least; everyone came to worship and bless the Lord.

As she reached the altar she stopped twirling and saw that it reached across the front of the platform, from one end of the room to the other. She watched as people knelt and cried before the Lord. *"Praise you Lord Jesus; we bless you Lord; thank you Jesus for your great love."* Voices of the saints were in one accord worshipping and blessing God. She began her ascent up the steps and noticed that behind the choir was a mural of Jesus riding a white stallion, descending from heaven with a sword in his hand approaching Jerusalem. Beneath the mural was a baptismal that was painted to look just like the river Jordan, and a plaque with the scripture which read.

16 For the Lord himself shall descend from heaven with a shout, with the voice of the archangel, and with the trump of God: and the dead in Christ shall rise first: 17 Then we which are alive and remain shall be caught up together with them in the clouds, to meet the Lord in the air: and so shall we ever be with the Lord.
(I Thessalonians 4:16 & 17)

She stood at the microphone and saw Holly, Molly, Mandy and Zeema sitting on the front row. They all smiled at Sarah. They had become very good friends through the years. Zeema had become a member of the church. Sister Matty Rose helped her move to the church a year ago. She ministered in music on special occasions. Sarah was touched to see her family all together in one place. Even Uncle George, Granny, and Grandma B were there. (It was a surprise for Sarah.) Sarah smiled and threw them a kiss as she stood on the platform. The church was packed with over three- thousand people. They came from as far away as Ashville, Charlotte, Atlanta, Mississippi, Jackson and of course Cedar Bluff. Everyone stood with their hands raised to heaven giving praise and glory to the Lord. Then a hush fell over the crowd. There were no introductions needed. Sarah with face uplifted, eyes closed, she began to sing!

I shall forever lift my voice to Calvary, to view the cross where Jesus died for me…how marvelous the grace that caught my falling soul…he looked beyond my faults and saw my need!

A slow, rising, crescendo, descended throughout the congregation like a wave. Higher and higher as if heaven had opened a window that sounded like thousands of angel voices being heard as they worshiped the King of glory; only the angels were silent. They were listening to humans give a resounding rush of rejoicing that exploded upward reaching into the Holy of Holies at the very dwelling place of God. This intrigued the heavenly host. Silence filled the room once more they waited, and then Sarah began to sing again.

Amazing Grace will always be my song of praise…for it was grace that brought my liberty, I do not know, just why He came to love me so. He looked beyond my faults and saw my need…. I shall forever lift mine eyes to Calvary, to view the cross, where Jesus died for

197

me… how marvelous, the grace that caught my falling soul… he
looked beyond my faults and saw my need.

Sarah's singing had taken her all around the world opening doors for her to tell her life story. Thousands of lives had been touched; whites and blacks alike, Mexicans, Asians, Greek, Japanese, Chinese, Italian's, and Jews. There were no barriers for her because she knew the creator of all human kind. Race did not hold her back. And she remembered her promise to Jimmy, to speak boldly. *Peace Like a River Church of God,* wanted to offer her a position as director of foreign missions. Her cousin Nick had accepted a pastorate position at the church four years before and he had recommended Sarah for the position. He knew she was returning from her tour. God showed him in a dream that she was the one to fill the position. When Sister Matilda Rose heard who he was talking about she didn't hesitate to write to Sarah. She knew Sarah was an answer to her prayers, she remembered the little girl who sang and witnessed to her years before. It was because of the anointing and obedience of Sarah that this church exists and now it was time to bring her back to finish the work God had for her to do in this place.

As the Holy Spirit moved on hearts, two hundred souls gave their lives to Jesus as Sarah sang *the Angel Song.* Sarah acknowledged the Holy Spirit and thanked Jesus for the opportunity to be a part of the experience.

Sarah prayed, "Lord Jesus you are the reason this church exists, help me to be your humble servant and do what needs to be done here."

Tears streamed down Sarah's face. Sister Matty Rose came to the microphone and said, "Brothers and sisters this is the young lady we've talked about over the years. This is Miss Sarah Evans, the angel girl. Everyone cheered as Sarah took the microphone again.

Sarah cleared her throat and said, "Good morning. What a blessing new souls for the kingdom of the Living God. Praise the Lord. I know you are new to this way of glorifying God but I don't think you're surprised by it. There are anointed men and women here to answer your questions and help you understand what comes next. Isn't that right Tim?" Sarah said from the platform. "I believe they are going to have you go to a special room for a little teaching session. You'll want to be baptized next. Just like Jesus." Sarah said as she smiled at the new babies in Christ.

Tim stepped forward and said, "Yes if everyone will follow me to the right of the sanctuary we have qualified, anointed people ready to assist you. It won't take long then you can be dismissed or come back and continue worshiping.

"OK great." Sarah said. Then she continued. "I'd like to take this time now to say that God gets all the glory. If not for Him no telling where I'd be today. Ever since I was a little girl, I've known the God of Abraham, Isaac and Jacob. He put music in my soul. I'm here to tell you today; God loves everyone. It's not the color of a person's skin, or who they know or don't know. It's the Spirit of the Living God that destroys the yoke of sin and sets the captives free through Jesus His son. Give Him praise, give Him glory…live for Him and tell others about His great love."

Praises rose throughout the sanctuary like the mighty roar of a lion. Then everything got quite again.

"God is so good! I want to thank you for having me here today God bless you all." Sarah stood before the congregation she poured her heart out to them. "I was raised by my Granny, Norma Jean and my Uncle George they're here today along with my Grandma B and Zeema, a very dear friend some of you may know her. My mama died giving birth to me and my daddy who was a Negro, was murdered the day after I was born. I grew up in Cedar Bluff, Alabama. I sing and I play the piano. I thank God he gave me such a special gift to use for him. I recently came back from a four year tour singing with the very amazing Mahalia Jackson." Applause went up at the mention of her name.

"Yes she is wonderful. We went all over the world it was something else. But I'm here today to a very special purpose. I've been asked to be the Foreign Missions Director and I received confirmation from the Lord when I received Sister Matty's letter. Yes, my answer is yes!" Everyone stood up and applauded. "Thank you so much I'm glad you approve. Stay in the spirit with me there's something God is asking me to do. I'd like to know how many children ten years old and younger are here?" The Holy Spirit was still moving. An usher stood up and said, "There's about 500 boys and girls, twelve and under in children's church next door. Do you want me to bring them over here?"

"Can you take me to where they are?" asked Sarah.

"I sure can," said the usher.

"Please keep worshiping I'll see you all again later." Sarah said. Stepping down from the platform she followed the usher. The service did not end. Someone else stepped up and continued in the worship.

Sarah followed the usher to the children's church next door. They were singing and praising God.

Sarah walked right up to the platform. She reverently stepped up to the microphone. "Praise the Lord, listen to me please, and get real quiet for a moment. Stay in the presence of the Lord but listen. My name is Sarah Evans and I have something special to say to you today. I'm going to be the new Director of Foreign Missions here but God wanted me to come over and ask if there are any mulatto's in the congregation?" About twenty-five kids stood up.

"I want the rest of you, if you don't know Jesus as your personal Lord and Savior to also pray when we say the prayer for salvation but only if you want too it has to be your decision. I will say that it's the best decision you'll ever make in your life. Please make your way to the altar and stand quietly. I know this is a little different this morning but God is telling me something and I need to tell you. God put this on my heart wherever I go because, I am also a mulatto. But that has not held me back from obeying the Lord. And you need to know this. Yes, the enemy has tried to stop me all of my life but God is greater. If God be for me who can be against me? Isn't that right? The answer is No One! I've been all over the world and I've found that all people are basically the same. We may have different cultures and beliefs but we are all the same. The differences are what make us unique. God has placed within each of us gifts and talents that he wants us to use for His glory. With that being said I want to do something here today that will change your lives forever and hopefully keep you for all eternity with the Lord Jesus.

Now of the ones who are mulatto, how many of you know Jesus as your personal Lord and Savior? Ten raised their hands. "How many of you want to know him?" The other fifteen raised their hands.

Sarah said, "Repeat after me; *Lord Jesus I'm a sinner but I want you to come into my heart and save me. I believe you are the son of God and that you were born of a virgin, you died for me on the cross, and you rose from the dead and you're alive. I ask that you come and live in my heart for the rest of my life now and forever. Amen."*

They all prayed. "Now, how many want to receive the baptism of the Holy Spirit and your prayer language? They all raised their hand. Sarah said, "Brother is there some anointing oil I can use? In case you don't know, the oil represents the Holy Spirit. The Holy Spirit is God's Spirit; He's part of the God-Head. There's the Father, the Son and the Holy Spirit. The oil was used throughout the bible.

Samuel anointed David to be king over Israel." *1 Samuel 10:1 – Says, Then Samuel took a vial of oil, and poured [it] upon his*

head, and kissed him, and said, [Is it] not because the LORD hath
anointed thee [to be] captain over his inheritance?

When people were sick they were also anointed with oil. *Is*
any sick among you? Let him call for the elders of the church; and
let them pray over him, anointing him with oil in the name of the
Lord: (**James 5:14**)

"Now that we've established what the oil is used for, let's
continue. While the usher is coming I want you all to kneel at the
altar but I don't want you to pray to receive the Holy Spirit I want
you to seek Jesus. Tell him how much you love him, thank him for
saving you and then graciously thank him for the gift of the Holy
Spirit and for filling you with your prayer language. Don't let your
mind get in the way. Sometimes you might get one baby word…if
you do, speak it out loud. The same way it took faith for you to
receive salvation just now, it takes faith for you to receive this gift.
It's already been given; all you have to do is accept it. Reach out and
receive it. It's as if someone is handing you a present. Accept it, it's
yours." Sarah said with confidence knowing in whom she believed.

Sarah anointed each one of them with oil then all of a sudden
the back doors of the church flew open and the children began to
speak in other tongues. Everyone was praising God, loving Jesus and
speaking in heavenly languages. They didn't even notice the back
doors. But people in the back of the church were astonished and
began shouting! It was glorious! One person spoke out in the spirit
and quoted "*John answered them all, "I baptize you with water. But*
one who is more powerful than I will come, the straps of whose

sandals I am not worthy to untie. He will baptize you with the Holy Spirit and fire." (Luke 3:16)

Sister Matilda Rose was standing in the back of the room she started shouting and giving praise to God. She stopped and told the ushers to bring the crippled children down front. But before she could get down front another child got up out of her wheel chair and started running around the church. The child's parents stared and praised God. Their daughter had not walked in five years. A little boy about eight years old, deaf and dumb from birth began to sing and praise the Lord. His mother shouted all the way to the altar.

Sarah stood at the microphone and praised Jesus. She looked up, lifted her hands and gave God all the praise and all the glory, then she said. "All you have to do is have faith in God, faith pleases God, and He honors faith. Jesus loves you and wants to give you another comforter to live in you and teach all about the Lord. The Holy Spirit is a real person He comes to reveal Jesus."

Kids begin to dance and sing and give worship to the Lord, each face shown with new light and hope and thankfulness. One parent said, "I don't understand it all, but this one thing I know my son was blind but now he can see. I don't need to understand it I want to praise God for what he has done for my son."

A tiny spark had ignited in the little community that sent a blaze of hope and new life as God's anointing fell on the *Peace like a River Church of God.* A revival broke out and went on for months. God moved as Sarah sang the *Angel Song.* People were healed, set free from cigarettes and alcohol. Lame walked, diseases vanished.

Reporters came to investigate the stories they had been hearing about. Skeptics came also but each time they came and didn't believe they left totally changed. God was doing a work not to give a show, he was saving souls; Sarah was an instrument who was willing and obedient to answer the call. And the confirmation of that call was the anointing that fell when she sang and told her story. Jesus was honoring His word with signs and wonders to all those who believed.

During the services Sarah stood before the crowds and began by singing and playing the piano. People were mesmerized by the sound. Then because of the anointing that was on her life, the Holy Spirit began to move and hearts would begin to soften, tears would flow and the Holy Spirit was free to move on the hearts and change lives that brought glory and honor to Jesus the son of the living God. By the end of summer the church had grown from 3,000 to over 5,000. They were coming in car loads not to see the amazing girl or hear her sing, although some were curious, but they wanted their miracle and left with more than they ever imagined. Salvation had come to them at, *Peace Like a River Church of God.* Over the next few weeks God poured out his Spirit on the people with miracle after miracle.

"So Sarah, after ministering these past months, do you still want the position?" Sister Matty Rose asked.

Sarah looked straight into her friend's eyes and without hesitation she said, "You bet I do! But I have a small request."

"What's that Sarah?" Sister Matty Rose asked.

"You remember Beth don't you? She'll be coming home from Africa soon. She's been there on the mission field for four years. I believe God is calling her to join us here too. I'd like her to assist me with this position. It's a huge job and I need some help." Sarah smiled as she asked Sister Matty Rose; she knew what her answer would be.

"Sarah you got it. I remember Beth and I've been following her ministry. As a matter of fact she's one of the missionaries that we support. So by all means bring her on board. God's already spoken to me about her. Is there anything else?" Sister Matty Rose said as she grinned and gave Sarah a big hug.

"No ma'am." Sarah said hugging her in return. "I think that confirms everything."

Beth arrived in the fall, she'd be home for a year and while she was home she'd be praying about whether she'd be going back to the mission field. Sarah had written to her about what was happening in the church and wanted Beth to come home but only if God was leading her. "God please give me the direction I need to be in your perfect will." Beth thought as she watched Sarah coming towards her.

"Beth, oh Beth you're here, you're really here. I've missed you so much," Sarah said as she grabbed Beth and gave her a great big bear hug. Beth returned the hug with as much love and affection as was given.

"I've missed you too Sarah." Beth said still holding onto Sarah.

Sarah could see changes in Beth she was a little slimmer her hair had grown far beyond her waist and her freckles were barely noticeable with the tan of her skin. But the most significant change was in her eyes. They glimmered with life and a confidence Sarah had not seen before. Sarah saw something else there too, but she wasn't sure what it was. A distance of some kind maybe, or a question Sarah would ask her about it later.

"Nick is preaching tonight. You'll be astounded at the wisdom God gives Nick when he preaches God's word." Sarah said walking Beth to her room. Beth was out of breath as she reached for the door. The staff lived on the church grounds it was home for them. Sarah had a room prepared for Beth. She'd be living there as well if she took the position. In the meantime she'd stay there while she was in town.

"Sarah I have to tell you something. Do you have time for a talk?" asked Beth, she was very solemn, quieter then Sarah remembered. Her best friend was always bubbly and full of life. She had the energy of a locomotive in full throttle.

Sarah's face became concerned as she came in and sat down, "What is it Beth? Is your mom alright? What's going on?"

"Sarah I have to tell you something but I'm not sure how." Beth said, exploring Sarah's face for acceptance and understanding.

"Tell me Beth, what is it?" Sarah was getting a little panicky.

"Ok, ok. You know how I've always dreamed of being a missionary and serving God on foreign fields? Well I had to come home. God did some amazing things while I was in Africa and I don't want to disappoint the Lord, but I discovered that Africa wasn't the place God had called me to serve. I've struggled with how to go about telling you this all the way home. Do you think I failed God?" Tears began to roll down Beth's face she drew in her breath and then the flood gates opened up. "Oh Sarah, I'm a failure. How will I ever be able to serve God again? How can I tell everyone? I feel awful." Beth couldn't look Sarah in the eye she felt so ashamed.

The demon of despair lurked at Beth's shoulder. Mockingly he sneered, *"Oh Sarah, Sarah what should I do? Tell me or I'll go insane. I'm such a failure. That's right you snibbling little fake, you're a disgrace. You'll never be anything more than a hypocrite."*

Sarah put her arms around Beth and let her cry for about fifteen minutes.

"Beth, look at me, are you through? I thought someone had died or had a horrible disease. I can deal with this. You are not…a failure. I've never seen you fail at anything. I've always looked up to you. You have always been there for me. I think you are the strongest and bravest person in the world. Why has this shaken you up so much?" Sarah reached for a box of tissues and handed one to Beth. Discerning the evil spirit, Sarah rebuked him in the name of Jesus in her mind. *The demon stuck his tongue out at Sarah; he was a little imp about the size of a mouse. Then he flew away out through the window and was gone.*

"Please look at me Beth. I want you to blow your nose, dry your eyes and stop this. God has a place for you right here and if you find this isn't His assignment for you then we'll keep praying until He shows you where He wants you. OK?" Sarah said beseechingly.

Beth stopped crying and took a deep breath she felt much better then said, "You're right Sarah; I don't know why it got to me. I felt like I was letting God down somehow and I was a little home sick. Africa was amazing but in my spirit it seemed as if God was telling me to come home. But I was confused. I mean of course He used me to win souls and teach music to some pretty awesome kids while I was there. But something was not quite right. I wasn't at peace in my spirit. It felt like something was missing, I was alone and everything was out of sync, doubt and despair began to wear me down." Beth sat and looked forlorn but was more at peace now.

"I know what you mean Beth the whole time I was on tour I felt the very same way. Like I was walking in a far distant place from where I was supposed to be ministering. Then I received the letter from Sister Matty Rose and everything fell into place. It's like the spiritual shoes finally fit. From the time we were ten years old and came to this place, God had a special plan for our lives I never dreamed it would be here of all places. Remember the dirt yard, the garage barely standing and all those dogs. I knew there was an anointing that hit here that night, but never dreamed God would build a church this big, did you? But He has and I believe this is where you're supposed to be too. But that has to come to you, from the Lord. I don't want to influence you. OK?" Sarah gave Beth a smile held her at arm's length and said, "Now where's my ferocious, on fire for God, friend?" Sarah said.

Beth was the only sister Sarah had ever known and she loved her dearly, but she wanted her to know God's will for herself. As much as she wanted her to be with her in this ministry she wouldn't do anything that would hinder her from being where God wanted her.

Beth stood up shook herself and said, "I'm right here and I'm not going anywhere unless God says differently. I will fast and pray to seek God's will for my life and hope he'll let me know very soon. Thanks, Lotto," Beth said as she felt God's peace settle in her spirit.

God's Call on Your Life

Make us glad according to the days wherein thou hast afflicted us, and the years wherein we have seen evil. Psalm 90:15

The next day Beth was asked to play the piano for the upcoming Sunday morning service and to speak on, *"Hearing the voice of God and how to know if you're being called to a foreign mission field."* It was ironic that this was the topic she was asked to speak about because Sarah had not said a word to anyone about their conversation.

"God what are you up too?" Beth thought as she read her assignment.

Early Sunday morning Beth had fasted and prayed for wisdom and guidance to know what music Jesus wanted her to play for the service. She was impressed in her spirit to play the traditional African tribal worship songs she had learned while she was in Africa. Dressed in her African dress and sandals, she made her way to the platform. Her fingers hit the key board and the next thing she knew she was caught up in a heavenly realm. There were thousands of angels surrounding her. The roads in heaven where she was, was

211

not paved in gold, they were dirt and rock but the dirt was florescent and the rock was crystal, but dull, not shiny. She was lifted up into the sky flying higher and higher. The sky was a blue she had never encountered and below was what looked like wild animals but there was no fear among them. They seemed happy and carefree. She could hear music but it came from everywhere at once from every direction. There were no speakers or buildings everything was total light but not blinding. "Lord Jesus, where am I?" Beth didn't speak the words, they came from her mind. One angel she saw was huge, maybe twelve feet tall, she looked young and happy. With long, golden, flowing hair that fell around her face and down her back. Her face was beautiful, fair and she glowed with light that was shining all through her being. Her eyes were not color; they were actually two bright spheres of light and when she looked at you, you felt genuine love. It was like she could see inside the deepest part of your heart but there was no fear. Her wings were silver and white, which protruded from the middle of her back, between her shoulder blades. They were about twenty inches above her head; the tips of her wings touched the floor. I'd say the wings were about 13' high with a 26' wing span. They fluttered softly about her, billowy, causing a gentle breeze when she spoke. A sort of misty halo outlined her body. She radiated with peace and joy. There was no fear she walked in perfect love. After a moment she sat down, her wings seemed too disappear then she motioned for Beth to come sit with her on a swing that was about 15 feet wide. The chain was a metallic orange and yellow material that hung in midair. It wasn't attached to anything. Beth had the thought of sitting on the swing and there she was.

"Beth, my name is Rose'el I am your guardian angel. I've been assigned to you since before you were born. I know you have some questions about your calling. Abba has asked me to answer any questions you may have." Her voice was like a melody, soft and gentle. She said that it off set my fiery personality. She had to be calm to handle my feistiness.

Beth asked, "Your name is Rose'el? Well Rose'el, I have been a little discouraged lately not knowing exactly what the Lords will is for my life. I thought it was to be on the mission field but I realized I was on the wrong assignment. What is my calling? Where do I belong? Is Abba upset with me for leaving the mission field?" Beth asked. She got a little carried away with questions in her enthusiasm.

"Alright Beth I'm a patient angel, let's take one question at a time, is that alright with you?" Rose'el asked in kindness but without using words.

"Yes of course." Beth said catching her breath. "And if it's alright with you I'll be using my words." Beth laughed and thought how silly I don't need to use words.

Rose'el gave a gentle nod of approval and said, "As you travel on your life's journey there are many assignments, many lessons to learn and then there is a specific assignment for you to carry out. For some it may only be one word given at a specific time and then their assignment is over and they come home. For others it could be a piece of music or art that is supposed to be created for a specific purpose. And for some it is a life time of ups and downs, twists and turns, lessons to learn, until they reach a specific time and date and then their assignment is over. Sometimes people get so caught up in their earth life that they forget there's an assignment to be completed. Along the way messengers or guardians if you will, help them get back on task. But when the ones that are called at a very young age are determined to please Abba and keep their awareness of his son Jesus; they are very sensitive to the Holy Spirits promptings and they stay on course their whole lives. You see Beth the purpose of earth-beings, Abba's-kind, is to bring glory to Abba. He made man-kind to love him. So to answer all your questions lil Beth, the father is very pleased with you. He loves that you recognized you were off task and He's happy you are aware of Him and that you want to please Him. So He has given you a very special encounter with the heavenly hosts. Beth, keep seeking Him, keep serving Him. You do that by serving others. This place that you and Sarah are a part of is a God place. He has a specific anointing here. That's why He used George to write the Angel song so he would bring you here at the age of ten. It was no coincidence. This place *Peace Like a River, Church of God,* is a safe haven for his children: The children that are here now and for the ones that are to come years from now. He placed its care into the hands of humble, loving, people. People He knew He could trust. He knew these people wouldn't use it for their personal gain or glory. That is why such miracles happen here. Their hearts are pure. And that is why He has assigned you and Sarah and Nick to this place. Do not be afraid to be a blessing here Beth. It pleases Abba when you are obedient to Him. Remember He loves you with an everlasting love. He will never leave you nor forsake you. Live for Him all the days of your earth life Beth; and you will never be afraid. You have the Holy one with you the Holy Spirit of Abba to teach you. And you have the Savior Jesus. He has given you His name to use to overthrow the evil ones. Never be afraid for Jesus is with you always." Then Rose'el took oil, it smelled sweet, the fragrance permeated the air then she poured it over Beth's head. She spoke in her heavenly tongue. Warmth flooded Beth's body inside and out. Peace that could not be explained flooded her being. Beth was anointed for her assignment. Strength and comfort settled in her mind causing total peace to settle over her.

It seemed like she had been away for hours but when she came to herself it had only been about five minutes. Everyone was praising God they had not even been aware that she had been away from the service.

Beth now knew her true assignment. All anxiety left her. She was no longer fearful or shaken that she had been a failure for leaving the mission field and no amount of badgering from the evil spirits would keep her from fulfilling the call on her life ever again.

From the balcony of the church, fear hissed and screamed but to no avail. Doubt screeched and jumped about. "Now what are we going to do, when Lucifer hears about this we'll be spending more time in the sweat box." They draped their sewer smelling, black maggot robes around them and vanished.

With all the praise and worship that was going on, evil could not come near.

Beth came to the microphone, she was refreshed and renewed in spirit, and then she began to speak.

"Brothers and sisters in Christ I've been asked to speak to you about *'How to know the Call of God on Your Life'* and *'How to know if you've been called to the Mission Field.'* First of all you have to know the King of Glory, the son of the living God, Jesus. Then you need to fast and pray and read God's word don't read it only, but study it. Paul said, in God's Holy Book, *'Study to show yourself approved unto God, a workman who needs not to be ashamed, rightly dividing the word of truth.'* II Timothy 2:15.

As you make yourself available to God and are filled with His spirit and His word, He will lead and guide you to your assignment. Most of the time you'll be searching for His perfect will by trial and error, but when you get your specific assignment you will be in total peace and confidence and you'll know. He will confirm it to you. And sometimes He'll even take you on a heavenly encounter and introduce you to your guardian angel. Be open to anything; God does not live in a box. He has been and will always be the creator of all things. He's everywhere, all at the same time. He knows the intents of your heart and He longs for a relationship with you. Talk to Him, then listen, He will talk to you of secrets and instruct you. He'll give you wisdom and understanding!

As a matter of fact, I had a God encounter sitting right here at this piano. I thought hours had passed but it was only about five minutes. I'm not going to go into the details because I don't want to bring attention to myself but I will tell you this. I now know beyond any doubt what my assignment is and where I'm supposed to serve. That's why I can stand up here right now and without hesitation tell you, when you know, you will know, praise God." Beth said.

"I thought I was in the perfect will of God when I was in Africa but something kept bothering me. I couldn't put my finger on it. I was in this tiny village, the people there are so open to God and sang with such joy in their hearts. Once they receive salvation they are the most loyal, dedicated and determined of any people I've ever seen. It was difficult leaving them, but I believed God had something different for me. As you seek God's face and perfect will for your life you will know, He will tell you and He'll confirm it to you usually with two witnesses. This one little girl her name was Sia, I'll never forget her, she looked at me and smiled, then she said, *Missy Beth it's time for you to go. God has something more for you in your homeland.*" God was speaking to me through her. She didn't know the turmoil I was having. But God's Holy Spirit did. He'll use anything or anyone to let you know. However you have to be open to hear His voice and obey Him when He speaks. He will confirm His word to you.

Pray, read God's word, be filled with His Holy Spirit pray in the Spirit and obey God. You do that, and God will show up. He will make Himself available to you and you will be doing His will." Beth said knowing something had changed in her heart. She had a Holy confidence that filled her soul. She was God's handmaiden, ready for service.

Praises went up like a roar all over the sanctuary. Again the Holy Spirit showed up and worship rang out as a sweet smelling savor that flooded heavens throne room right into the very presence of Jesus, the son of the living God.

The Baptism

Let thy work appear unto thy servants, and thy glory unto their children. Psalm 90:16

"Brothers and sisters we are gathered here today to baptize those who have recently came to know our Lord and Savior, Jesus Christ." Sister Matty announced as she stood in water waste deep in the baptismal.

Several lines of white robed men, women and children stood waiting their turn to be submerged in water. They were making an outward show of an inward commitment, to live their lives as Christians and follow Jesus's example.

Tears streamed down each face as one by one they entered the water and rose with smiles of gratitude and thanksgiving. Laughing and praising God they were forgiven of their sins and forever set free!

John Jackson was first, and then Mary and Tom Barnett took their turns. The Smith family all eight of them followed suit. The baby, little Gracie was four years old.

Holding Gracie in her arms, she was completely awe struck. Sister Matty said, "Gracie Smith, do you believe Jesus died for your sins and has forgiven you and lives within your heart forever?"

Gracie putting her arms around Sister Matty's neck pulled her close and kissed her on the cheek, then nodded, "Yes."

"Sister Matty," Gracie said in her little girl, boisterous voice, "Can I send Jesus a kiss too?" Before Sister Matty could answer, Gracie put her hand to her lips and threw Jesus a great big kiss. "NOW I'M READY AND YES I KNOW JESUS LIVES RIGHT IN HERE!" She pointed to her heart. She spoke so loud that everyone in the church laughed and applauded.

Matty laughed as she held Gracie in her arms she said, "I baptize you in the name of the Father, and of Son and of the Holy Spirit." Then she submerged Gracie in the water. When Gracie came up, out of the water she was speaking in her prayer language. Shouts of joy and laughter broke out everywhere.

Nick began to prophecy by the power of the Holy Spirit, *"Yes a little child shall lead them and whosoever asks of me shall be filled with my Spirit. They will overflow with joy, peace and love. Let not your hearts be troubled you believe in me, believe also in my Father for it is He who has made all things for his good pleasure. This is the beginning of blessings never look back; always look to me, says the Lord. I am the way the truth and the life."*

Two hundred and fifty people were baptized. And a hundred more were saved that day. God is faithful, His word will be accomplished.

Sarah and Beth led everyone in praises to God as they sang and worshipped until midnight. Pillows and blankets were given so that whoever needed to could stay the night. The next morning people were still glorifying God. A revival broke out that went on for two months. As a matter of fact it is still going. Just like in the early Church, God was adding to the Church daily. The Holy Spirit was on the move!

New Sunday school teachers were given positions. Ushers, deacons, Youth pastors and Assistant Preachers and teachers were trained to participate in the ministry. God had a plan and His plans were carried out in great detail. There were miracles and mighty works, signs and wonders that God was with them. This ministry was truly orchestrated by God.

"We are growing leaps and bounds." Sister Matty said. "We're gona need to set up a meeting with the leaders to teach the new converts. Many of the new members are being spiritually attacked by the enemy. We need a prayer team for special prayer times too, so they'll have around the clock reinforcement. Mandy will you call your mama and Aunt Holly, and the three of you set up the prayer teams? You're going to need a lot of help." Sister Matty said as she headed out the door of her office.

Mandy was more than willing to help at any time. "Yes Granny I'll call right now."

Matty, hurrying out the door, looked back at her granddaughter and said. "Thank you sweetheart, I knew I could count on you."

Mandy had been serving the Lord for as long as she could remember. At fifteen she didn't know anything other than Church life and she was perfectly content to serve in any way she could.

She picked up the phone and dialed her mama. "Hey mama, this is Mandy. Granny needs us to get the prayer team together. Yes the enemy is attacking the new babes in Christ. Yes, right away. Will you call Aunt Holly for me? OK great, I'll talk to you later. I love you too. Bye."

She didn't pay any attention to people's stares or whisperings. She'd never thought much about it. She'd always been accepted for who she was. Her mama and aunt and Granny never mentioned it so she grew up thinking she was just like them. She was strong and bold. She looked more like her daddy than her mama but it just didn't matter.

Mandy tidied up the office and kept herself busy doing her chores.

Sarah came into the office saw Mandy and asked, "Hey Mandy, do you know where your Granny has gotten off too? I need to ask her about the prayer team."

"Yes ma'am," Mandy said dusting the bookcase; she looked up for the moment and said, "She's gone on an errand she didn't say where she was going. She was in a big hurry though."

"Will you give her a message for me?" Sarah said looking around for a pen and paper to leave a note.

"What's that Miss Sarah?" Mandy said handing Sarah some paper and a pencil.

"Just give her this note and I'll check back with her this afternoon." Sarah leaned over the desk and wrote her a note.

"Sister Matty, Please see me as soon as possible; I need to talk to you about one of the new converts. It's extremely important. Sarah."

Handing the note to Mandy, Sarah said, "Thanks Mandy I'll catch up with her later."

Mandy gave Sarah a hug and said, "Alright, I'll see that she gets it as soon as she gets back."

"Thank you Mandy. Do you need help with anything?" Sarah asked hugging her in return. "You look a little flushed."

"No ma'am, I'm fine. I just have some things on my mind but it's nothing urgent." Mandy looked down at the feather duster she was holding, twirling it in her hands. It's nothing. I'm fine."

Sarah said, "Well if you're sure it's nothing, because I'm always available to talk if you need too."

"Thanks Miss Sarah I'll keep that in mind." Mandy blushed and stepped back a bit then said, "Well you see, I'm fifteen and there's this boy that I like but he's a year older than I am. His mama said he couldn't talk to me. I thought it was because of our age. But I found out it's because I'm…well you know, mulatto. I told him I'm as white as he is, but he just laughed. I was furious. That's the first time in my life I ever thought much about it. What would you do Miss Sarah?" Mandy was flushed, her hands were sweaty and she just swung that feather duster around and around.

"Oh Mandy, I'm so sorry that happened to you. Sarah said and knew exactly how she felt. "I've had lots of encounters with those kinds of challenges. It never goes away. But as we grow in the Lord it doesn't hurt as much. You're still young; I know that doesn't help much because it hurts when others are cruel. My Granny always told me they're just ignorant and don't know any better. There'll be lots of people like that in your life. I learned that I had to forgive them or it would drive me crazy. I will tell you this. There will be someone special one day that will rock your world. And it won't matter one bit about the color of your skin. Your feelings are important Mandy and I'm here for you whenever you need me. But don't let this guy or his mama get the best of you. I heard this saying the other day. "Go where you're celebrated, not where you're tolerated. And I thought, you know what, that makes a lot of sense."

Mandy stopped swinging the duster and said, "That makes a lot of sense to me too. Thanks Miss Sarah, I feel so much better now. I'll give Granny your note. I love you Miss Sarah." Mandy said and calmness settled over her.

Sarah pulled Mandy close, gave her a big squeeze and said, "I love you too Miss Mandy, see ya later alligator."

Mandy laughed and said, "After while crocodile."

Granny came in a little while later. Mandy looked up from a book she was reading and said, "Here's a note from Sarah, Granny; she said it was urgent that she talk to you."

"Thanks baby girl, I'm on my way for a staff meeting right now, and I'll talk to her there." Granny said as she grabbed her notes and headed back out the door.

Mandy went back to reading her book.

The Love of a Friend

*And let the beauty of the Lord our God be upon us: and establish
thou the work of our hands upon us; yea, the work of our hands
establish thou it. Psalm 90:17*

Beth reached for the phone as it began to ring. "Hello, yes
this is Beth. Tommy, how are you? Great! Yes I got back last week.
Of course come by any time. OK, that sounds good see you then."
Beth was excited, blushed and smiled to herself. She had, had a
crush on Tommy ever since grade school. "I wish he was here right
now." She thought as she came out of her room and headed to the
main conference room. Nick, Sarah and Sister Matty Rose were
holding a staff meeting. Beth was invited to attend the meeting as
well.

As Beth entered the room she saw Nick sitting to the right,
then Sarah. Sarah motioned for Beth to come sit next to her. Sister
Matty Rose said, "Come on in and take a seat Beth. Everyone, I want
you to meet Beth she is our newest member to the staff. She's been a
missionary to Africa for the last four years. Please be sure to
introduce yourself and say hi to her after the meeting."

Beth nodded and took her seat. There were about 108 men and women gathered in the room.

Sister Matty said bringing the meeting to order, "Everyone I want you to know I had a conversation with Sarah a few minutes ago. There's a spiritual warfare going on; the devil is mad and with good reason. God is moving. The Church is growing. Souls are getting saved and miracles are happening. We need to increase our prayer time. Pray in the Spirit. I've asked Mandy, Molly and Holly to set up round the clock prayer teams. Sarah has confirmed this is much needed. One of the new converts was asked to leave his job today. They didn't want religion being preached at his office. All he did was pray over his food. So with that being said, let's pray steadfastly that God will give him a better job. Nick, will you lead everyone in prayer before we get started?" Sister Matty Rose knelt down by her chair to pray. She never stood when she went into the presence of the King.

Nick looked toward heaven and began to pray, *"Holy Father God, we come to you in the name of your son Jesus Christ of Nazareth we ask that you wash us and cleanse us from all unrighteousness. We bind every hindering spirit, every thought, deed or action that is not pleasing to you and we ask that the precious Holy Spirit give us wisdom and understanding so that everything will be done orderly with your grace and peace. Let us work together in love and harmony. Keep us in one accord to obey your word so that souls will be brought into your Kingdom. You said in, (I Corinthians 4:20), for the kingdom of God is not in word, but in power. We are*

here to build your kingdom, Father. As it is written in your word,
*(**Zechariah 4:6**), Then He answered and spake unto me, saying, This*
is the word of the LORD unto Zerubbabel, saying, Not by might, nor
by power, but by my spirit, saith the LORD of hosts. Not by might, nor
by power but by your spirit, Lord Jesus. So we ask you to give us
strength to overcome the enemy, you overcame him and you gave us
the Holy Spirit to help us in this world. Just as you said long ago in
*(**Matthew 17:21**), this kind goeth not out but by prayer and fasting.*
Help us to pray and help us as we fast for your will to be done. Let
us not fall asleep but be watchful and ready at all times. Satan goes
about as a roaring lion seeking whom he may devour but he has no
power over us, he's a toothless lion. We need your power Lord, keep
us in the palm of your hand. We've gathered here today to seek your
face and humble ourselves that we will be faithful to the call you've
given us. We ask that you give our brother a miracle, a new job one
that will be better than the one he has and one that will bring glory
and honor to your name. Help us all to do our part, in the name of
Jesus. Amen and Amen."

Sister Matty blew a kiss toward heaven then stood and said, "Ok here we are there's one hundred and eight of us here today the Holy Spirit gave us a plan. We're going to need each and every one's cooperation. The church has grown to astronomical proportions but God wouldn't give us this job if He didn't know we could handle it. So we need to make some minor adjustments and proceed forward with this holy calling. I know we have administrators and God inspired leaders in this room so here's what I want you to do for me. We've put together some packets of information regarding where we need people to serve. I want groups of twelve to gather together and each group take a table. You'll see a card with the name of a fruit of the spirit at each table. In your packet you'll see the spiritual fruit you have been assigned too.

There is; Love, Joy, Peace, Longsuffering, Gentleness, Goodness, Faith, Meekness, and Temperance; this is the fruit of God's Spirit, which is written about in (**Galatians 5:22-23.**)

With twelve people at each table and nine fruit, one at each table we have a total of 108 exactly what is needed.

Now I don't want people to feel like they are separated from one another we are all to have this fruit in our lives, it is not fruits it is one fruit with many facets this is God's character....This plan will help us keep everything organized. The bible says to do all things with decency and order.

So at the table of love, table of peace, etc., there should be twelve people gathered there and then set up teams of two at each table. There should be husbands and wives together or if you're single two single people together. God always sent them out in two's. The same goes for all the other tables as well. Also we had buttons made up with the appropriate fruit for each group. You will be responsible for ushering people, helping at the altars, working in the parking lot, balcony, kitchen, nursery and children's sanctuary. We are going to organize the same thing for our children's church as well. We have some very responsible young people so why shouldn't we train them to serve as well. This is what it's all about.

So at each table of twelve, for example the table of love, you will have two team members that total twelve working together and will be called 'the fruit of the spirit of love table.' All of you (Love) will be assigned to work at the altar and you'll have your buttons so you'll be recognized by everyone. Does everyone understand? Alright then is everyone at their table? Good. This is very important. The Holy Spirit impressed me to tell you that the fruit of the spirit is extremely important. There are going to be brand new baby Christians who don't know anything about being Godly or how to be filled with the Holy Spirit. So it is imperative that we set the example and show the fruit of the spirit to everyone who walks through our church doors or who walks on this property. Not just here but in our homes, at the grocery store even if we travel out of the state we are to be examples of God's family. We are always to show God's love, joy and peace, longsuffering gentleness, goodness, faith, meekness and temperance and it should be that way in every part of our lives. This is what the plan is all about." Sister Matty Rose said as she raised her hands to heaven and gave praise to the Lord.

Then she continued; "Now in the old testament God gave Moses and Aaron instructions on how to appoint leaders over the twelve tribes of Israel. Because there's over 5,000 people attending here each week and many through the week we need strong, faithful leaders who are to lead, not to control. With that being said I want our five pastors and their wives to stand right where you are so we can anoint you with oil and pray over you." Pastor Joshua and

Rebecca Edwards serve the orphans and widows; Pastor Daniel and Hanna Rogers serve the elderly; Pastor David and Maria Long serve the children; Pastor Nick Williams serves the singles; and Pastor Stephen and Josie Hart serve the homeless (foster kids) and disabled. They all stood.

"Let's all gather around them and pray." Sister Matty began to pray.

"Pastors, you are the leaders God has chosen for such a time as this. Answering your phones at all hours of the day, visiting the sick and praying for them, this is a huge challenge but you've got the Holy Spirit to help you, pray in the spirit and delegate, delegate, delegate. There are lots of lay people in the church that also have gifts and talents and want to be used by the Lord. You will oversee the nine *Fruit of the Spirit Administrators*. And organize which group is assigned to their various stations. Everyone has to work together for the kingdom of God. Remember souls are at stake here. The Spirit of God has kept at bay the demons but they are very real and they want to strike any way and anytime they can. Stay prepared, keep your armor on and stay in an attitude of love and forgiveness. Now if there are no questions you may all be dismissed. Also, remember to set up your appointments on your calendars to meet on a weekly basis. We want to be ready for Sunday morning service. Make sure you wear your buttons. Flyers will be pinned up all around the church and grounds so new people will know who to go to if they need assistance. And remember too, that everyone is important and nothing is too small a request. Use wisdom. God bless you all." Sister Matty Rose then left to go to another meeting.

Beth turned to Sarah and said. "Sarah before you go I want you to know that Tommy is coming to see me today at 2:00. Do you want to get something to eat with us? You and Nick are invited." She said as she gathered up her materials.

"Really, that would be great! Did you tell Nick?" Sarah asked. "You might want to catch him before he leaves. I'll meet you in the cafeteria at 2:00." Sarah had another meeting she had to attend.

"Great, I'll see you then." Beth said and headed out the door to catch Nick.

Nick was walking towards the door as Beth caught up with him. "Hey Nick are you doing anything around 2:00 today?" Beth asked.

"Nothing I can't change for you Beth." Nick had a big smile on his face. "What's up?"

"Tommy's coming for a late lunch, will you join us? I asked Sarah too, she said she'd be there." Beth said with excitement and anticipation on her face.

"Well sure, I'll meet you guys at the cafeteria at 2:00. I can't wait to see the Senator." He said with a little laugh. "By the way, is it OK if I bring a date?" Nick said then blushed, but his sideways grin was so cute she let it go.

"Well sure after all we need to meet whoever the lucky lady is. If you're bringing her she must be someone very special." Beth said in her bouncy, confident way.

"She is very special and if she'll have me I'm going to ask her to marry me. But don't say anything to anyone freckles." Nick said with happiness all over his face. "I haven't asked her yet."

"My lips are sealed Nick. I'm looking forward to all us being together again. I won't hold you up any longer I know you have important places to go and people to see. Catch ya later Pastor Nick." She said playfully.

Nick went out the door, "Yeah see ya later, Bouncy."

Beth went into the sanctuary to pray but as she did a girl about fifteen years old stopped her and asked, "You're Miss Beth aren't you?"

"Yes, yes I am. Can I help you with something?" Beth looked at the girl. She was petite, slender frame, short brown hair and hazel eyes. She wore the typical bell bottom jeans, bright colored top and peace-sign earrings hung from her ears. Then Beth noticed a bruise on the girl's cheek.

"Can I talk to you?" the girl asked. "My name is Debi Anderson; Pastor Steven Hart suggested I talk to you." Debi was a little jittery and kept tucking her hair behind her ear as she looked down at the floor.

Beth looked closer at the girl but didn't stare. "Of course let's go where we can have a little more privacy." Debi followed Beth to a small conference room. As they entered the room Debi threw her hands to her face and began to sob.

Intimidation, fear and suspicion clung to the girl, their talons dug deep into her head and back. Beth discerned the demon spirits; she put her arms around Debi and began to pray, casting the demons out, she commanding them to leave.

The demons began to scream, vile green, slimy saliva, spewed from their mouth, "You can't do that, she's ours, and she'll always be ours."

"Debi," Beth said, "say thank you Jesus for setting me free."

Debi repeated the words, and then she raised her hands and praised Jesus. "Thank you Jesus, thank you Jesus, I am yours, I am yours."

Beth spoke directly to the demons, "You have no authority here I command you to GO! I plead the blood of Jesus over Debi Anderson right now in the mighty name of Jesus. I bind you and cast you out!" The demons gave one last hiss and let go, they screamed and shouted, chains held their putrid hands and feet, and then they vanished.

Debi felt peace for the first time in her life. She clung to Beth, stopped crying and totally relaxed. Then Beth said, "Now we can talk freely."

Debi sat at a table, looked at Beth and smiled shyly. "I don't know where to start Miss Beth. I've been abused since I was eight years old. My mother left when I was three and then my dad died when I was five. I was sent to live with my grandmother, but she couldn't take care of me so a social worker from my school had someone come and take me to a foster home. The home I was in had five other kids all older than me. It's hard in a home everyone looks out for themselves. I was constantly picked on and then Mr. Barnes made me…Debi began to shake; head down she threw her hands to her face and sobbed she couldn't finish her story.

"It's alright Debi you're safe now. No one is ever going to hurt you again. Beth said as she put her arms around Debi and let her cry.

When the tears subsided Beth asked. "Where are you living now?"

"I, I ran away from the last shelter. I've been staying in an old shed not far from here. I saw a flyer about the church and something urged me to come here. Pastor Steven was handing out cookies a few days ago at the Pig, that's a local grocery store. He also gave me a bible. He had a big smile on his face he looked so kind and for some reason I trusted him. I took the cookies and the bible. He asked me where I lived and my name. At first I was suspicious then I watched as he helped a boy and how he talked to everyone. I told him I was afraid and needed some help. He told me about the church and said to look for a lady with red hair and lots of freckles. I knew it was you when I saw you. He said your name was Sister Beth."

Beth laughed. "Yeah well I don't mind my freckles or my red hair anymore. In fact my childhood nickname is freckles. But you can call me Miss Beth." She said with a chuckle.

"I'll have to do some research on the foster care system it may take me a couple of days. In the meantime, I'll take you to meet Pastor Matty Rose she's the overseer here and will know what to do about getting you a safe place to live." Beth was thinking.

"Oh no, Miss Beth please don't send me back to the authorities. They'll put me back in the system and I'll be lost. Please don't send me back." Panic, fear and terror struck Debi's heart it was seen on her face she looked around for a way out of the church.

"Debi, listen to me, I said nothing is going to ever hurt you again and I mean it. But I have to let Sister Matty Rose know what's happening. She's a wonderful lady and she won't put you in harm's way. I'll be with you the whole time. OK?" Beth spoke real soft and put her arm around Debi's shoulders.

Debi calmed down for the moment. "I'll go with you right now and we'll meet her. If you don't want her to help you after that we'll think of something else." Beth was kind but stern. She knew she couldn't let her stay on her own it was too dangerous.

"Alright but if she says anything that looks like she's going to send me back I'll run so fast no one will ever find me." Debi said.

Beth prayed silently. "Jesus I need your help guide me Lord, she's your' brand new baby girl please keep her in the palm of your hand. Amen"

Fear screamed out, "No more praying, I can't take this. I'll come back when the girl is alone and vulnerable." He vanished leaving behind a vapor of red dust which dissipated leaving a smell of rotten eggs behind.

236

Debi and Beth looked around, "What's that awful smell?" Debi asked.

Beth knew what it was. She'd encountered it many times on the mission field. She just dismissed it. "Come on let's go find Sister Matty Rose."

Sister Matty Rose was in her office she was finishing up her devotion and put it aside when a knock came on the door.

"Come on in the door is open." She said setting her glasses aside.

"Beth come in, come in. And who is this lovely lady?" She asked with her usual happy smile on her face. Love radiated from her countenance.

"I'm sorry to disturb you sister Matty Rose. I know you're very busy." Beth said.

"Oh don't worry about that Beth my door is always open. Come right in." She motioned for the girls to come in and have a seat.

"Thank you ma'am, this is Debi Anderson." Beth continued to say. "She gave her heart to the Lord about thirty minutes ago. She's a beautiful person but life has treated her pretty rough. She's in need of a place to live. She's been in the foster care system since she was about five or six years old. Her mother left her when she was three and her dad passed away when she was five. She lived with her grandmother a little while but she couldn't take care of her. The system was not kind and she's been abused. She's been living in a shed not far from here. We've got to get her someplace safe, Sister

237

Matty Rose, we can't send her back. Can you tell me what we can do for her?" Beth was determined that if they didn't have a safe place for Debi to live that she'd get a place herself and take care of her. She gave her word.

"We get lots of cases like this all the time and thanks to our legal services here at the church we have a place set up for children who come from "the system." Don't you worry Debi we're going to help you." Sister Matty said with a reassuring grin. "Father God loves you too much to abandon you. Who is your social worker? I promise you will not be going back there. You're going to have to trust me. I know that is a hard thing to do but if you look within your heart you'll see I'm telling you the truth." Sister Matty Rose smiled and waited for Debi to answer.

"You really promise you won't send me back there?" Debi needed to know without a doubt that Sister Matty Rose could be trusted. She was adamant she would not go back to the foster home, she'd run away first.

"I really mean it. As a matter of fact the facility is right here on campus. I'll take you to see it right now if you like. I bet you could use a hot shower and some food, am I right?" Sister Matty Rose said as she stood up and held out her hand to Debi.

"Yes I'm starving and a bath sure would feel good." Debi took Sister Matty Rose's hand and said. "I bet it would." Then she said to Beth. "Beth its 11:00 a.m. if you want you can come with us and I'll show you everything too. This will be part of the ministry you'll be assisting with. I know it is one of your callings." Sister

Matty Rose said and was very understanding when it came to someone in need of ministry. "Come on girls follow me."

The facility was set up for fifty kids, twenty-five boys and twenty-five girls from the ages of five to seventeen. They were also tied to adoption agencies so children were always coming and going. There was constant supervision, with an on-campus honorary mom and dad who lived in the dorms. Lizzy and Dave Lamplight, a couple, about forty-five years old, devout Christians, never had children of their own but have a love and compassion for homeless kids.

Beth looked at her watch and said, "Oh my how the time has flown I have a lunch appointment but I'll be checking in on you from time to time."

"It's OK, Miss Beth I feel very safe here. You go on I'll see ya later." Debi was calm and knew in her heart that these people could be trusted.

At first it was difficult for Debi to become settled but in a week's time she began to adjust to the routine perfectly. Her school grades improved, her self-esteem picked up and she even began piano lessons and was quite good. She had a natural talent and played by ear. She was asked to become part of the music team in teen church and accepted. She also helped the younger kids when they first arrived and made them feel safe. She was truly blessed for the first time in her life.

At 2:00 pm Beth, Sarah, Nick, Angela (Nick's bride to be) and Tommy met for lunch. Nick introduced Angela to everyone.

"She goes by Angel." Nick said.

And they could see why, she was a beautiful lady. Her strong southern drawl made her that much more adorable. "It's nice to meet ya'll. Nick has told me a lot about you and I feel as if I know ya'll already." Angel said as she shook each ones hand. What she lacked for in her petite size she made up for in personality. The minute you met her you instantly became friends. There was compassion and trust in her almond colored eyes. And her smile was as sincere and captivating as her beauty. She moved with grace and confidence and she could look right into the deepest parts of your heart with her penetrating eyes. The gifts of discernment and healing were operational in her but she used wisdom when speaking and listening to whoever was talking. Everyone could see how much Nick was in love. He didn't have to say a word he was giddy and shy and attentive to her every need. He had it bad. And from the looks of her she felt the same way.

To take the spot light off of them Nick asked, "How long will you be here Tommy?"

"Only today, then I'm headed back to Washington DC. I wanted to meet with you guys because we are going to pass a bill that I think will be beneficial to your work here. I wanted to get your input and hopefully get a date with Beth." Tommy said with a smile and gave Beth a wink.

"Well that's no problem at all; I'd follow you to the moon if you asked me too," Beth said as her face glowed which made her freckles brightened to a deep rose color.

"You two are too much, why don't you tie the knot and get it over with." Sarah said jokingly she had no idea that is exactly what he had in mind.

Tommy got down on one knee pulled out a box opened it and presented a 2k diamond ring that shot out sparkles in every direction. Holding it out to Beth he said, "Beth, will you marry me?"

Beth dropped her fork, Sarah choked on her drink as it came out of her nose and Nick sat there like a Cheshire cat, he knew that was coming. Angel smiled.

"Wha…what!!!!!!" Beth said having the breath knocked out of her.

Tommy raised his voice, "I said, Beth, will you marry me and make me the happiest man on the planet and beyond? You have to know how I feel about you. Writing you every day while you were away, calling you every chance I get. I love you Beth Montgomery. Now what do you say?" Tommy held out the ring, and his breath waiting for an answer.

"Yes! Yes I will!" Beth shrieked. Jumping up from their seats they all hugged each other. Fireworks seemed to burst all around them as the joy spilled out onto everyone.

Then Beth said stammering as everything ran through her mind all at once. "There's one tiny challenge; we will have to wait two years. I have some obligations here to complete; I signed a two year contract with the church."

"That's not a problem. All I needed was a commitment from you I will wait the two years, but after that you're going to be my wife forever." Tommy grabbed Beth, kissed her passionately and said, "Set the date right now because I won't wait a minute longer than that."

"Well, I've always dreamed of having a summer wedding so it can be outside. I think June 18, 1973, would be a very good date. Maybe we'll have a hippie theme. Just kidding. I don't even know what day that is but that's the date. It's also mine and Sarah's birthday." Beth said with excitement and a little bit of delirium in her voice. She was beaming.

They all agreed. "Sarah you will be my maid of honor of course."

"Of course," Sarah said.

"And Nick will you be my best man?" Tommy asked.

"You bet I will." Nick shook Tommy's hand enthusiastically.

"Well now that, that is decided, I have to run and catch a plane. I'll call you later sweetheart." Tommy said. "It was nice meeting you Angel I look forward to seeing you around for a very long time." Tommy winked at Nick and said. "You're next buddy." They all laughed.

Beth and Tommy embraced and gave each other another passionate kiss. Nick and Tommy shook hands again, Sarah gave Tommy a huge bear hug and then everyone said their good-byes.

The next morning Beth had to be at the Home for kid's facility to meet the staff and to organize her committee. Mr. Rick Stevens stood in the hallway waiting to meet his new boss. Beth came around the corner and smiled. "May I help you," She said.

"Hi, my name is Rick Stevens I was hired yesterday. You see I was fired for praying over my food. Sister Matty Rose said she was looking for someone to help out at the Home for Kids. So here I am." Rick said rushing as he told her the story.

"Well God did do a miracle. We just prayed for you last night. Praise the Lord. We can certainly use the help. Welcome aboard. Come on in I'll show you the ropes. I'm new myself but we can learn together." Beth shook Mr. Stevens hand and was thrilled how fast God works.

"We'll need to set up some schedules for breakfast, lunch and dinner. In the evenings homework will need to be completed before watching television. Kitchen duty will be assigned on a rotating schedule. The older kids can help the younger ones get ready for school each morning and with homework each night. For free time, there is a library, a swimming pool and TV shows rated for general audiences only. That should keep us pretty busy. Attending church is not optional. Everyone will need to attend the service. The only time they're allowed to miss is if they are terribly sick or if there's an emergency. Oh yeah, and there are unscheduled fire drills given once a week. The kids will love it. Coming from their backgrounds there shouldn't be a problem." Beth said as she gave Mr. Stevens notes and instructions walking throughout the facility.

Rick Stevens placed his notes in his briefcase, taking everything in as Beth talked. He took a breath and said, "I just want to say thank you and please let everyone who prayed for me and my family know that I don't know what I would have done if this job had not been available. I'm a new Christian and I love the Lord with all my heart. I won't let you down." Rick was tall, about 6'2. His smile was contagious. He had the light of the Lord all over his countenance. He was perfect for this job.

Beth looked him square in the eye and said, "Rick you're a God send. God always knows what's best for us and somehow He always works everything out for our good. You'll be great. Thank you for coming. Will you be living on campus?"

Rick turned and said, "No ma'am. I have a home not far from here. My wife and son will be staying there for now. Maybe later we'll be able to move here but not right now."

"Well I'm sure it'll all work out. Are you hungry? Let's go to the cafeteria and get some lunch. I'm meeting some friends. You're welcome to join us if you like," Beth said heading for the door.

"Thank you Miss Beth but I'm meeting my wife and son, maybe next time." Rick said as he ran ahead and got the door for her.

"Ok sure, next time." Beth thought how nice he's a gentleman.

Over the next few days everything went pretty smooth and then a boy named Devon Spencer arrived.

Devon was twelve years old; his parents were drug addicts which had overdosed leaving Devon on his own for over a year. When social services got him he had been living in an abandoned trailer. He had sores and scabs all over his body. He was withdrawn and never looked anyone in the eye. He'd jerk his head around constantly making sure no one could see him. He ate whatever he could find in trash cans. His eyes were two hollow dark pitted sockets that stared out from a narrow, drawn face. His teeth were rotten and a scar reached from his right eye brow down to his chin, where a rat had eaten part of his face. Devon was nearly dead, when Pastor Nick came across him. He had been visiting a new member of the church and noticed a horrible stench. He knew that smell from the ghetto he'd ministered in for three years. So he looked in the abandoned trailer and found Devon semi-conscience.

Pastor Nick visited him in the hospital every day for a week. After he learned Devon's story he signed for him to be placed in the, *Peace Like a River Home for Kids*. He knew there would be a whole lot of challenges but he also knew God was bigger!

Lizzy and Dave assigned three seventeen year olds, Tracy Parker, muscular, 6'1", blond hair and blue eyed jock. Everyone loved Tracy. Rick Cooper was short and stocky with red hair cut in a flat top style with green eyes and full of mischief. He loved to wrestle and had lots of energy; and last but not least, Dale Bailey he was a baseball star or so he hoped to be one day. Slender frame an extremely fast runner; his sandy brown hair and brown eyes made all the girls giddy. When he smiled his straight white teeth sparkled, and lit up his face with a dimple on each side of his mouth that melted your heart. These boys made a great team even though the system beat them up pretty bad. Meeting Jesus changed their attitudes and their lives. They loved helping others and it showed in their leadership. They are the captains who oversee the boy's dorm for the twelve year olds.

It was midnight all lights had been out for hours. There were night lights all along the corridors and bathrooms but there must have been a power surge everything was pitched black. Screams loud and shrill came from somewhere down the hallway.

Tracy, Rick and Dale sprang from their bunks grabbed flashlights and started running down the hall.

"What's going on?" All three boys said at the same time.

"It's Devon; he's on the floor screaming," Billy said. Billy is 13, small for his age. He has kinky black hair and black eyes that match his skin, he was assigned to help with Devon; the boys share the same room. "He's been restless all night. When everything went black he started screaming, rolled out of bed, I couldn't see anything. Then you were here before I could call for help." Billy said looking from one boy to the other he was quite shook up.

"OK, thanks Billy take this flashlight and go call Pastor Josh. We're gona need to get the lights back on. We'll take care of Devon." Tracy said.

Rick and Dale were attending to Devon. "Calm down buddy it's alright we're right here with you." Rick said bending down to reach for Devon.

But Devon threw a punch and hit Rick in the face. He began thrashing and kicking he was having a seizure.

"Billy, tell Pastor we're going to need the doctor too. Thanks man and hurry!" Tracy, Rick and Dale had been trained for these kinds of emergencies.

"Dale, grab his pillow and place it under his head. It shouldn't last long. The main thing is to make sure he doesn't hurt himself." Tracy said pointing the flashlight at the bed.

Devon began to settle down, he stopped jerking and his breathing became stable. Fifteen minutes later Pastor Josh, Lizzy and Dave came running into the room. Then the lights came on.

"What happened?" Pastor Josh asked.

He saw Devon lying on the floor sleeping peacefully at that point.

Tracy filled them in on what had happened.

"The doctor will be here in a few minutes." Pastor Josh said making sure Devon was stable.

Dale had been praying silently.

Doctor Riley arrived assessing the situation he said, "Let's lift him back onto the bed I don't think it's going to bother him. He seems to be in deep sleep."

After checking Devon to make sure he was alright, Doctor Riley said, "I'm going to need to run some test on him. Can you bring him to the office tomorrow? I'll let my staff know we need it STAT. He should be fine until then. But we don't' want to take any chances. It could be more serious than we think. Let's just make sure."

Pastor Josh being a take charge kind of man knew how serious the situation was and said, "We'll make sure he gets there doc."

"Alright you all try to get some rest." Doc Riley said as he gathered up his medical bag. He was anxious to get back to the hospital.

Pastor Josh looked at everyone and said. "Thanks guys, you did a great job tonight. Now try to get some rest. It looks like we've got our jobs cut out for us. I'll see you in the morning. Billy, I'll stay here the rest of the night so don't worry about anything. You get some sleep too, Lizzy. And Dave thanks for your help."

Lizzy said, "Thank you Jesus for getting us through all this. Amen."

Dave grinned and said, "Yes thank you Jesus!"

The next morning went according to plan and Pastor Josh took Devon to the see Doctor Riley. Devon was weak but stable; he was light as a feather he couldn't stand up, so they got a wheelchair. "Devon we've got to fatten you up, what you need is some meat and potatoes." Pastor Josh said tousling the boy's hair. But Devon didn't respond.

They decided to admit Devon to the hospital. They ran test after test and waited for the results. Three days went by. Flowers filled his room and cards from the kids at the facility were taped all over the walls. Devon was in a kind of coma his eyes were open but he didn't respond. A psych analysis was completed and after five days they received all of the test results.

Sister Matty Rose, Pastor Josh and Doctor Riley met in the doctor's office.

"Devon is going to need a whole lot of care; he will never be like other kids. He won't be able to communicate or walk or feed himself. He has severe neurological damage to his brain and a rare blood disease caused from the rat bites. It will be a miracle if he lives another six months. I'm sorry, but Devon is not going to make it." Doctor Riley said with an elusive, detached tone in his voice.

Doc Riley was a middle aged man of about 58. He was apple shaped, bald and wore round frame glasses. Every time the doctor spoke his eyes would squint and then he'd breathe hard through his nose. He didn't believe in Jesus, he was obnoxious and had the personality of a porcupine.

"Well that's what you say Doctor Riley, but I have a God who does miracles." Sister Matty Rose said full of faith and confidence.

"Now Sister Matilda Rose, I know what you're going to say, but let me assure you this is very serious. Devon needs twenty four hour, seven days a week care. We can't allow him to be disturbed by a bunch of bible thumping, fanatics disrupting this hospital." Doctor Riley said. "You know my stand on all that hoopla!" Doc Riley squinted and snorted.

"Please call me Sister Matty Rose, doctor. And you can say what you want to, but I won't be moved by your mumbo jumbo." Sister Matty Rose said with a determined and concrete no holds barred faith in the living God attitude. Even bull dogs had to give up when she set her mind to something. It wasn't stubbornness that gave her that strong will, it was in knowing who she belonged to, and that God had come through for her too many times and nothing or no one could shake her lose from the God of the Universe she knew in whom she believed and was persuaded that nothing would move her from Him!

The 24-hour prayer warriors were praying for Devon and for Sister Matty Rose. God was about to turn Doctor Riley's world upside down and inside out. He may call himself an atheist but God had other plans for the dear Doctor. Plans, the good doctor had no idea about nor could he control. This was the beginning of miracles for Doc Riley.

Because Sister Matty Rose had legal custody of Devon she was the one who said what kind of care could be given to the boy. The hospital had to adhere to her wishes and legally the hospital could not dismiss him as long as the bill was being taken care of, which it was.

Visiting hours were from 9:00am to noon and from 2:00pm to 4:00pm then from 6:00pm to 9:00pm seven days a week.

Sister Matty Rose called for a staff meeting and said. "I've called everyone here this morning for a very special reason. As you know one of our children Devon Spencer is very ill. The doctor is saying he has only six months to live or less. But we serve a God who is alive, who says, if we ask anything in the name of Jesus, believing we will receive it. We've been given a huge opportunity to receive a great miracle. Not only a healing for Devon but salvation to come to our good Dr. Riley. God has laid it on my heart to call for fasting and prayer. I need forty people who are up for a challenge. We will be fasting and praying for forty days. The fast will be clear liquids only. We will be staying in the sanctuary during this time with no disturbances of any kind and while we are fasting, Sarah and Beth will be at the hospital ministering to Devon. Whoever the Holy Spirit is talking to right now about doing this raise your hand." Sister Matty Rose looked around the room at the 108 people. They all had their hands raised.

"I knew God could count on you all but we only need forty, the Lord was very specific. Those of you that have the gift of healing come stand to the right of me. There were exactly thirty-nine and with Sister Matty Rose that made forty. Now the rest of you may also fast and pray but these specific ones will be staying in the sanctuary for this appointed assignment." Sister Matty said.

Pastor Daniel and Hanna Rogers were among the ones chosen. They also had the gift of administration so Sister Matty Rose said to them. "Please make all the arrangements as quickly as possible we need to start this tomorrow morning."

Doctor Riley stood at the foot of Devon's bed looking at his chart. "There's no hope for him, none." He thought to himself. There was a demon of disgust and anger standing at his side. Doubt and unbelief whispered in the doctor's ear. *"Look at him he's a goner, no one can help him now. Just pull the cord no one will see."* Death *laughed and said, "yeah come on d o c t o r you can do it."* Mocking

251

and lies were pressed close to the doctor's face, "there is no God, no miracle worker, and no good fairy to save him."

Matthew Riley had given his heart to the Lord when he was ten years old at summer camp. But when his father and mother were killed in an auto accident, Matthew turned away from God and vowed there is no God. If there was he wouldn't have taken his parents from him. His guardian angel stayed with him all his life and tried desperately to bring him back to the Lord. He stood there now watching and spoke to Matthew's heart. *"Don't listen to them God loves you and God loves Devon. God didn't kill your parents a drunk driver full of bitterness and hate hit them head on that night. There was nothing that could be done. Your parents loved God and are with him now. Don't do this, Matthew its murder." But Matthew couldn't hear his angel Simkah pleading with him. Matthew looked at the respirator then at Devon but something inside of him said that would be murder, you'd lose everything you've worked for.*

Billy, Devon's roommate, was praying for Devon. "Lord Jesus please protect Devon let your holy angels surround him right now and keep him safe."

The demons screeched and screamed out, "Noooooooooooooooo, stop that child from praying! Send in legion." *But God said NO!* Billy's prayer was answered. A host of holy angels were dispatched to Devon's side, swords drawn, the demons ran as the heavenly warriors pierced the demons putrid scales of thick hide, they could not escape. *Screaming and bloody they wreathed in pain and torment. "Please, please stop; go away; send us into the swine not the abyss! Not the abyss!"*

Michael the Archangel sent the final blow and yelled, "Go, into the swine and do not come back." The demons foaming at the mouth cried out and vanished.

A holy cheer rang out as the warriors high fived each other and danced around the tiny frame of a boy who was struggling to survive. Even the demons around the doctor were swept away. They couldn't stand in the presence of the holy party that was going on. For a few moments the doctor felt surrender and a kind of hope. Then he let his mind be taken again by doubt. He left the room disgusted with what he had been thinking.

The next morning Sarah and Beth arrived at the hospital. The nurses were given strict instruction by Dr. Riley, "Do not let anyone from the church disturb Devon."

The forty prayer warriors began their prayer vigil they were all in one accord. At exactly 9:00am the doctor was called away from the hospital to visit one of his other facilities. There was a staff change. The doctor's instructions did not make it to the new nurses on duty. Sarah and Beth walked right into Devon's room. Beth brought a portable keyboard with her and Sarah began to sing the angel song.

> *Though times are hard*
> *I'm by your side*
> *Your tears I hold within my hand*

No matter what I'll hold you close

Look to the one who understands.

Though fears may come and tears may fall

Be still and know that I am God

Let perfect peace restore your heart

And know my love we'll never part

Chorus:

I walked the road of trials and torment

I sat with those who love me still

But on the cross

I felt the suffering of all the ones who love me most.

The birds they sing a nightly chorus

Of joy and peace to all they bring

So lift your voice and head toward heaven

And learn their song, their song and sing.

He gives me peace, He gives me life, the angels sing be glorified

Praise to the King our mighty King

We're going home on angels wings.

When in the stillness now at midnight

I see the star of love so bright

I'll never ever doubt my Savior

For He will lead me through the night

And on the breeze I hear Him whisper…

Press on my child and do not weep

For at the dawn you'll have your answer

So close your eyes and go to sleep.

Chorus:

I walked the road of trials and torment

I sat with those who love me still

But on the cross

I felt the suffering of all the ones who love me most.

The birds they sing a nightly chorus

Of joy and peace to all they bring

So lift your voice and head toward heaven

And learn their song, their song and sing.

He gives me peace, He gives me life, the angels sing be glorified

Praise to the King our mighty King

We're going home on angels wings.

Sarah's voice penetrated the hearts of everyone that was in the hospital. A holy peace settled over the patients, nurses and visitors. They listened as Sarah sang the anointed ballad. That was day one. For the next forty days Sarah came each day and sang the song. Dr. Riley had been called away every day at the same time. The prayer warriors prayed God was moving. On day forty Sarah began to sing. But Dr. Riley was in the building his appointment had been canceled.

Nurse Jenkins, "Who is that singing?" Dr. Riley asked.

"Oh Doctor don't you know? It's Miss Sarah from the *Peace like a River Church of God. Nurse Jenkins said enthusiastically.*

The doctor looked at her dumbfounded. "Well tell her to stop. She can't be disturbing all the patients, this is highly uncalled for." The good doctor was beside himself. Conviction hit him like a steel bat grabbing his head he winced in pain.

The demons scrambled, "We've got to do something if he hears the song he's a goner, all of our hard work for the last thirty years will be for nothing. Call in the big boy, hurry... Anger, do something." Anger gripped the doctor's head tighter. Pride landed on the doctor's shoulder and Fear was right beside him.

Pride sneered, "Doctor Riley what is everyone going to say when they find out he's your patient." Fear chimed in, "Oh no, you can't allow that, you'll be a laughing stock."

Simkah, drew his sword, "Not this time you toothless lions, you're headed for the fire pit." And with one swift swing their heads rolled on the floor. They swooped down grabbed their heads and ran for cover. *Death sneered disgustingly and said, "You win this round but it's only a matter of time...I will return one of these days"...his sinister voice let out a war cry that shook the building, then darkness carried him to another dimension he was swept up and out of the room.*

A beam of light showed on Devon's face and he stirred. The fasting and prayer had worked the demons scattered. Dr. Riley fell to his knees crying like a baby and prayed. "Oh God forgive me, I've been a fool. I've been wrong all these years. Please forgive me Jesus, forgive me."

Sarah kept on singing; Beth kept on playing the key board and praying. Devon opened his eyes and sang along with Sarah; for forty days he had heard an angel singing and he sang along with her, only this time he was conscience. The harmony was amazing. His voice along with Sarah's brought a miracle to the hospital. People, in comas were waking up; heart monitors were going off because they weren't needed. Chemo and radiation stopped, cancers were healed. And salvation came to Dr. Riley. Sunday morning Dr. Riley was sitting on the front row and Devon was sitting right beside him. Devon was healed completely even the scar across his face was gone. Dr. Riley started adoption paperwork to make Devon his son. In the morning service, Sarah was called to sing she called Devon to the platform to sing with her. Tears ran down each face as the song rang out in the church. A little boy had been sentenced to die; he had no parents or anyone he could turn too. But God knew him. He turned ashes into beauty and gave him an earthly home and an eternal home as well. All for the love of a friend! Greater love has no one than this, than to lay down one's life for his friends. (**John 15:13)** (NKJV) There was a special place in Sarah's heart for the unloved, the suffering and dying; she spent her life ministry serving others.

"Sarah, what will you do today?" God asked.

"Lord what would you have me do?" asked Sarah.

"Sing for me Sarah, sing the *Angel Song*." God's light shot out in every direction as He smiled.

Sarah closed her eyes and sang out through heavens portals. *Philomel spread her wings wide as she glided to the floor and escorted Sarah into the throne room. She smiled, stood to one side for Sarah to walk ahead, and said, "After you Sarah."*

A procession of angels stood with their wings spread out creating a radiant canopy over Sarah as she walked past each one. There was Rose-el, Sage, Garth, Stephan-Arrow, Zarta-el all the guardians of her life. Fifty generals, seventy musicians and one hundred infantry angels gathered on each side of the golden street; bowing their heads as she walked past. Showing honor and gratitude to a servant of God! A life lived in service for His Majesty the King of Kings and Lord of Lords. Everyone in one accord began singing The Angel Song as Sarah entered into the very presence of the Lord!

She looked at her hands there were no wrinkles or crooked fingers from the arthritis; she stood without being bent or in pain. She didn't hesitate she was giddy, she was young, her skin wasn't brown or white…it glowed with the radiance of the master. Twirling in a dance of tremendous joy she could not contain her happiness. Her pure white **robe** an abundance of fine linen flared out in a circle around her like a ballroom dancer, she abandoned all thought of self …suddenly realizing she was in the presence of a heavenly host, she stopped. Standing before her was a glorious throne. Cherubim and Seraphim fluttered around the throne joyfully. The music was energizing as it permeated the air around her. Then everything got very still. Sarah threw herself, face down on the floor as she recognized the master. Jesus, whose heart was full of love for her, said, "Welcome home Sarah we've been waiting for you! Please stand up." He held his arms open to receive her. Sarah jumped up and ran into his arms hugging Him for the longest time. She kissed the scars in His hands and bowed to kiss His feet. Tears of joy and thankfulness ran down her checks her heart was filled with overflowing gratitude as she praised the Savior.

"Jesus, Oh Jesus, it's you, it's really you." Sarah's words were almost breathless as she held her hands to her chest then combed her hand through her hair with unbelievable excitement.

Jesus, touched by her gesture, took Sarah by the hand and said, "Sarah there's some souls here who want to meet the girl who sang the Angel Song. It touched and changed their lives. They said that if you had not sang that song they would have never been here."

Sarah looked at Jesus then to the souls waiting to meet her. She wiped the tears from her face and tried to compose herself. She smiled and stood very still then said, "Yes by all means I'd love to meet them." One by one Sarah was welcomed by a host of family and friends, some she had never met before. There was her mama, and her daddy; Granny, Uncle George and Grandma B.; Zeema and Sister Matty Rose and of course Mayor Johnson. Sarah hugged each one as more tears, but tears of joy, ran down her face.

"Mama…daddy…." Sarah could not contain her joy. They ran to each other and embraced.

Sarah's mama said, "We've waited a long time to finally meet you Sarah. We are so proud of you. Your life has been a glory to the Lord. You truly are an Angel Princess. And now we have eternity to spend together."

Her daddy handed her some of heaven's wild flowers, colors so bright and beautiful they shown with the glory of the Lord. Everything glowed. Sarah gave them both a big hug.

"Yes eternity." Sarah said as the fullness of joy flooded her soul.

A little girl waited patiently to shake her hand. Her name was Abbey. She said, "Miss Sarah I listened to your song on the radio and asked Jesus to come into my heart. At that very minute a bomb went off in our building and I was killed. If I had not heard you sing that day I wouldn't be here."

"Sarah, my name is Yared you visited my country, Israel. I came to hear you sing. I was a devout Jew and kept the law. My very good friend Ibrahim invited me to come hear an American mulatto girl sing. I was curious, so I went. I could not help myself. Before I knew it I was asking Yeshua into my heart. I just want to say Rav todot (*thank you very much*.) I'm here today because you sang." Yared said in his strong Hebrew dialect, he shook Sarah's hand vigorously.

"Hi Sarah, my name is Tara. I was a prostitute. There was no way I was going to set foot in a church full of hypocrites. They'd shun me and run me out of their towns. All I wanted was a warm bed and a little something to eat. But this one day, a man came to the corner where I was working. He smiled and said, "Young lady do you know Sarah Evans?" I thought to myself, 'What kind of line is this?' Then I thought, 'I know what you want mister why beat around the bush.' But there was something different about him. He didn't want sex; he genuinely wanted to know if I knew Sarah Evans. I looked him over and said, "No mister I don't know any Sarah Evans." He handed me a record and said, "Listen to this. No strings attached, just listen." Then he turned and walked away. Two nights passed. I had been sleeping in a rundown room in back of a tavern. I picked up the record and took it to Mr. Jones's bar. He had a record player and said I could use it anytime. I put the record on and heard an angel sing. It was you Miss Sarah. You were singing the Angel song. Before my mama died when I was seven years old, she used to take me to Sunday school. She died; I went to live in an orphanage. I ran away at fifteen. I was hungry so I sold myself for something to eat. I knew it was wrong but I didn't know what else to do. I knew about Jesus but I thought I was too dirty to even say His name. But when I listened to your voice there was something about the words you sang, '*Though times are hard, I'm by your side, your tears I hold within my hand, no matter what, I'll hold you close, look to the one who understands.*' I was twenty by then and life had been cruel. I lost a baby and almost my life. As I heard the words to the song, I fell down on my knees and cried uncontrollably. Jesus saved me that very minute. I went to a local church and the pastor and his wife took me in. I got clean and lived for fifty years ministering to the prostitutes of that city. And because of you singing the *Angel song* I led a lot of ladies to the Lord. There's a whole choir right over here because of your song Miss Sarah. I just want to say thank you. I'm so glad I met Miss Sarah Evans that day, but most of all I'm glad Jesus saved me."

Sarah gave Tara a great big hug, and waved to the choir and said. "Tara, thank you. I'm glad I got to meet you too!"

People were all waiting to welcome her with warm hugs and inspiring stories, it was a wonderful reunion. Sarah was touched and had no idea the impact she had, had, on so many people. Her heart was full, she kept saying. "Thank you, it wasn't me I give all the glory to Jesus. I was just doing what He called me to do."

Jesus listened to everything that was said. Then He turned to Sarah and said, "Sarah, you were obedient to my call and because of that, many souls were saved. It's OK to receive honor. Your humble heart and unpretentious spirit are two things I love about you. Well done my good and faithful daughter."

Sarah touched by everyone's warm welcome said, "Thank you Lord. I'm speechless and grateful for every soul that is here and I'm thrilled that I obeyed your call in my earthly life. I wouldn't have changed it for anything."

Sarah looked at Jesus and said, "Lord, there's someone I desperately want to see." She scaled the crowd of faces searching, hoping. "You know who it is Lord. I lost him so long ago." As she spoke, Jesus nodded for her to look over her right shoulder. She turned and saw him. Jimmy was standing there watching and waiting, then their eyes met. Jimmy had a great big smile on his face and said, "Welcome home Lotto!"

Sarah let out a sigh and shouted with great joy and exuberance, "Jimmy!!!" Sitting there beside Jimmy was her faithful, loving friend, Taffy; she stood up, wagged her tail and ran to Sarah with a stick in her mouth ready to play fetch! "I knew you'd be here." Sarah said. "Come on girl." Taffy gave Sarah a great big wet kiss and said, "We've been wait'n for ya." Sarah's eyes grew wide; and with a great big smile she threw her arms around Taffy and said, "I knew animals could talk."

Sarah's homecoming was complete.

Eternally happy ending!

"I am Alpha and Omega, the beginning and the ending, saith the Lord, which is, and which was, and which is to come, the Almighty." (Revelation 1:8)

"THE KING IS COMING!"

I hope you enjoyed reading Sing Sarah Sing. It was a blessing and a pleasure to write.

If you don't mind I'd like to ask you to take just a moment and go to Amazon.com and give 'Sing Sarah Sing' a review. I greatly appreciate your input, God bless you on your journey.